WHO CRIES FOR MOTHER EARTH

A NOVEL

MARGARET HINES

WHO CRIES FOR MOTHER EARTH

A NOVEL

This is a work of fiction. Any similarities to real names, places or events are purely coincidental.

www.BringsGood.com

Published by Brings Good, LLC
c/o CMI
4822 South 133rd Street
Omaha, NE 68137

Paperback ISBN: 978-1-7326807-1-5
Mobi ISBN: 978-1-7326807-2-2
EPUB ISBN: 978-1-7326807-3-9

Library of Congress Cataloging Number: 2018954752
Cataloging in Publication Data on file with the Publisher.

Cover Illustration by Conrad Hinz, artist and graduate of the Corcoran School of Art in Washington, D.C.

Publishing and production by
Concierge Marketing Inc., Omaha, NE

Printed in the USA

10 9 8 7 6 5 4 3 2

For our beautiful and
precious Earth Mother

FOREWORD

Who Cries for Mother Earth, by author Margaret Hines, is a life-refreshing spiritual experience for readers of all backgrounds, ethnicities, and religions. It's a story of a young *Lakota* coming into her own in the mentorship of her *Unci* (Grandmother), who is a medicine woman, a holy woman, a healer. Yellow Bird Woman journeys through the camps of her people on the Northern Plains, in the woods, prairies, and fields gathering herbs and roots that are the age-old traditional medicines of her people. And she takes us into the spiritual world of the Vision Quest where she learns of the potential of goodness in a world of peace and love; but she also foresees the devastation of humanity and Mother Earth brought on by greed and hate and selfishness.

Each of the short chapters begins with a poetic prayer of supplication in which the young holy woman asks *Wakan Tanka* to give her strength and guidance in serving her people's spiritual and physical health.

The book is fiction, but is based on *Lakota* culture and spirituality. It presents a woman's perspective in what has long been seen and portrayed as a man's world of spiritual power and wisdom.

CHARLES E. TRIMBLE, OGLALA LAKOTA

INTRODUCTION

I am Yellow Bird Woman.

There are times when a vision is so powerful it can rest in a person's soul forever. This is how it happened for me. I was born in the mid-1800s when the winds of blizzards challenged all living things in the sacred Paha Sapa (Black Hills) of South Dakota.

As a young woman, I was given the vision while in deep spiritual practice and at the exact moment of the conjunction of a crescent moon and two planets. I knew the vision was a gift from the Creator, and honored it in my heart. After much prayer, I was told to give the vision to the people.

To be born a human being is a magnificent gift from Wakan Tanka (God). To be given a purpose and a direction in life to help others is a blessing from the Divine. To understand human suffering with compassion is to begin our own healing and the understanding of ourselves and our place in the world.

Sometimes it takes more than one lifetime to even get a glimpse.

(Publisher's Note: For Lakota translations and pronunciation guide, please refer to a glossary at the back of the book.)

OH CREATOR, HAVE compassion on me

I cry for a vision

I will not ask without giving

I will sit on a hill

Without water and food

I will open my heart to You

I will pour out my praises

I give myself to You Creator

Show me my life's purpose

My reason for being here

That I may help in some small way

The peoples' suffering on Earth.

My name is *Zintkala Zi Win* (Yellow Bird Woman). I was born in the time the *wasicu* (white men) were appearing on our lands. We were in the revered *Paha Sapa* (Black Hills) of South Dakota. My love for the blessed hills was so deep within my soul that I longed to always be there and feel the majesty. To hear the winds blowing through the pines was to be enveloped within the heart of Mother Earth herself.

We were the *Lakota Oyate* (Lakota People) and we were free. We walked the ways of *Ptesan Win* (White Buffalo Calf Woman.) We were known to all the tribes as the peacekeepers and givers of the medicines. We were a warrior people who were strong physically and spiritually. We walked with inner peace and joyfulness.

Winter could be difficult, but it was also a time of calm reflection and uplifting prayers. The people made winter camp to endure the harsh winds and blizzards of blinding snow. Everything stopped when the storms arrived. The people looked ahead to the upcoming *Wiwanyang Wacipi* (Sun Dances) and *Hanbleceya* (Vision Quests) of the spring and summer and took heart.

I came into this life on the wintry winds of flying *wa* (snow) and cold frost. Our camp was in a little valley surrounded by pine trees. Our family's tipi was warm with a dancing fire in the center and heavy buffalo hides covering the outside. The fire cast twinkling flickering shadows on the sides of the tipi. My Mother and I were wrapped in a buffalo robe while she held me close. I felt her deep love for me after being with her for nine long months, and was comforted by the rhythmic beating of her beautiful heart.

Within a few days, her warmth began to fade, and I could no longer hear her heart beating. She became very ill and did not survive child birth. For the rest of my life, I longed to know her and to hear her soft singing voice again. As a little infant, my Mother's Mother, *Unci* (Grandmother), took me inside the *Inipi* (Sweat Lodge) and held me tightly as she prayed over me. The *Inipi* calmed me and I felt safe. Perhaps it brought back the warm memories of the Mother who so loved me and could not stay with me.

My Father tried to take good care of me. He was gone long periods of time because he was a great warrior and hunter. *Unci* took me with her when he was gone. My Father continued to struggle with parenting until I was one. One day he was quickly called to be part of a war party while *Unci* was away doing a healing. He quickly took me to the orphan's tipi where I remained for several days.

When *Unci* returned, she found me in the orphan's tipi and decided it was time for me to come live with her. She told me that my Father was a very good and brave man, but the orphan's tipi would be no more. She took me to live with her where I remained until I was a grown woman.

Unci welcomed my Father to see me and take me places. I loved it when he came to visit. He was fun and played games with me and taught me how to ride fast on a pony. I was a small child when my Father quit coming to see me. *Unci* told me he was very brave and honored by our people, but he had to go with my Mother up in the sky. She told me he would always watch over me just as my Mother had. I didn't think I could live without seeing my Father. I still longed to see my Mother. I wanted to go to the sky so I could be with them. I begged *Unci* over and over to please let me go to the sky. She assured me that one day I would go to the sky, but to remember they would come down from the sky and watch over me. I dreamed of going to the sky many of my young years.

Unci was now my Grandmother, my Mother, and my Father. After losing my parents, she doted on me day and night and began teaching me the spiritual ways.

She kept me very busy, and I learned and grew in the ancient ways of the *Lakota*.

Unci lived with an older woman, *Unci Oma* (Grandmother Other). They were both known to the people as wise medicine women. They were healers and seers and advanced spiritual beings. My two grandmothers took turns caring for me. *Unci* took the greatest responsibility of raising me. I was with her most of the time. She taught me at her knee how to do the medicine work and how to comfort people. Each of my grandmothers had slightly different ways of working with the medicines, and I learned from both of them.

My grandmothers were the most wonderful gift to me. I learned their ways and delighted in the light of their wisdom and teachings. I was like a small sunflower nurtured with special medicines and shown how to praise the Creator. *Unci* wanted me to be a beautiful open flower for the work of *Wakan Tanka* (God).

As I grew, I too became a *Lakota* healer, seer, and medicine woman who forever followed in the wise footsteps of my adored *Unci*.

HEAR ME SPIRIT of the medicine
Hear my prayer to you
I ask not for me
Only for your sacred medicine
To heal another who is sick
Hear me spirit of the medicine
I respectfully ask
For your most precious blessing
Oh, hear me spirit of the medicine
I humbly call you.

From the time I was a small child, *Unci* and I gathered the *pejuta wakan* (sacred medicines). We took large baskets and went out almost every day from spring through fall. Even in the winter time we could pick some of the medicines. *Unci* brought food and water for us and made the gathering of *pejuta wakan* a special time.

Unci called the medicines and sang for them, or danced for them, or prayed for them. Since we moved our camp from time to time she didn't always know where she could find the *pejuta* she needed.

Unci taught me to listen for the spirit of the medicines once we had called them.

"Listen," she told me. "They will tell you where they are. They want to help. But always remember they are very *wakan* (sacred). Approach them humbly and respectfully. Ask them if they want to help before harvesting them. Maybe they're not ready. They will tell you."

With *Unci's* careful instruction, I too began to hear the *pejuta wakan* call me. Each one had a different voice. Some had deep voices, and some had high voices. Others had distant voices or delicate voices. My heart seemed to flutter when I heard them, and I patiently waited for their ethereal tones. My love for them and their beautiful joyful sounds profoundly deepened in me as I matured.

Unci taught me to harvest the plant medicines. We carefully cut some plants and left their roots so they could grow back. When we used the roots of other plants, we took the very mature ones and left plenty of other roots for future growth. Whenever we harvested any part of a plant, we said a prayer and thanked the medicine in the plant for helping us. Then we laid down sacred *cansasa* (red willow bark) to show the medicine our deepest respect. As we prayed we said "*wopila*" (thank you) to the plant for giving us its *pejuta wakan*.

Each day after gathering, there was more work to do as we brought the *pejuta* back to our tipi. All the grandmothers helped with the precious medicines and were quite prayerful and joyful as they handled them. Some of the plants were hung to dry in the sun and could be kept through the winter. Bark from large bushes had to be preserved within a few days of picking. The grandmothers stripped the chokecherry sticks and the red willow sticks of bark and let them dry in the sun. Other medicines were aired out away from the sun.

The gathering of the *pejuta wakan* was very important. My grandmothers gathered medicines not only for our family but for many others. Our *Lakota* tribe doctored all the other tribes for many miles, and traveled to them usually once a year. We were *wolakota* (peaceful). We were the doctors and spiritual advisors to the plains. It was very important to have the right medicine for the sicknesses that presented themselves in each person.

Unci and *Unci Oma* were highly revered with the people. They took care of many things. Not only did they tend to sicknesses of the body, but also sicknesses of the mind and sicknesses of the spirit. Both of them were very spiritual, but I always thought my *Unci* was the most advanced. As I grew older I began to realize what power she had. She was heavily protected by the spirits who honored her for doing the medicine work. She was never bothered by wild animals when we were out digging the *pejuta wakan*. Some would come near, but they would retreat upon seeing her. Others would come near to talk with her.

Unci taught me how to listen for an animal that had a message. Sometimes the message was a healing for a person we were praying for. Other times the animal wanted to help Grandmother in some way with a vision. Yet however they came, the animals were regarded with special respect. *Unci* taught me to be very still and listen out of my "other ears" when they approached us with a message.

I was still young when a *tahca* (deer) came out of the forest and stared at me. Instantly I knew this deer was different. She stood and looked at me while staying very quiet. I heard her, but her lips did not move, her head did not bob, her ears did not twitch. I just suddenly heard her in my mind.

"You are growing in wisdom every day," the *tahca* began. "I will bring you beautiful visions and hopeful words for your life. I will guide you and give you direction and spiritual advice. I am your spirit animal and I am always with you. Remember. Remember."

As she turned away, I realized tears ran down my cheeks. My heart fluttered as it did around the *pejuta wakan*. I felt joyful and free. I wanted to run fast and be free to jump bushes like she did. I wanted to run to her and be with her. Powerful feelings rushed over me from the *tahca's* visit, yet I stood still knowing this was *wakan* (sacred) and I needed to be respectful and humble. I fell to my knees in deep gratitude.

"*Wopila* (thank you)," I called out to her as she ran back into the forest.

"*Wopila. Wopila. Wopila.*"

Unci found me by the edge of the forest praying and praising *Wakan Tanka*. She taught me that sacred plants and animals had direct connection to Him and so I listened to the *tahca* with my soul and my very being. I told *Unci* what had just happened, and she listened, smiling and nodding at me.

"*Zintkala Zi Win*, you have received this blessing with grace, humility, and in a very respectful way. I knew your spirit animal would appear to you, but I didn't know when. She has arrived long before I thought she would. You are still very young, but this is a sign that we need to give you our teachings faster than we had planned. In order for these teachings to come to you, humility and respect must be present in you at all times. I believe you are now ready to go forward and receive these blessed teachings. Do you believe you are ready? Can you commit to this?"

I deeply believed in the ways of *Ptesan Win* (White Buffalo Calf Woman) and all the teachings *Unci* had given me. I knew that if I honored the sacred plants and animals and the direct blessings from *Wakan Tanka* that came through them, they in turn would honor me and help me with healings for the people as they did my Grandmother.

"Yes *Unci*," I replied. "I am ready and will commit to this beautiful way that you have taught me."

"*Waste'* (good)," she replied. "We honor the sacred plants and animals with every part of our lives, and in turn, they honor us and our people and give us blessings that are beyond our ability to imagine them until they are bestowed upon us."

"*Waste'*," I replied as joyful trembling spread over my body.

3

WHAT DO I give
That sacred Lakota ways
Will work through me
To help the people
I am human
Imperfect and selfish
Will I learn
The kind of deep humility
That must be felt
In all areas of my life
Or will my mind keep
Taking me on enticing trips
Away from my inner self
Away from my very soul
Oh Creator, have pity on me
I pray for your help
That I may see what is truly real.

The *Lakota* people were known to other tribes as big brothers. We traveled from tribe to tribe and helped with doctoring and our spiritual teachings. Our instructions were from *Ptesan Win* (White Buffalo Calf Woman). We were to teach and help others with all the knowledge and blessings we had been given.

Traditionally it was said that we followed the Tatanka Oyate (Buffalo People) in a wide circle that took us from our sacred Paha Sapa (Black Hills) to the far northlands and then to the distant Southwest. It took almost a year to complete the circle of *tatanka* (buffalo).

In recent years as the *wasicu* (white man) came to our lands, we did not make the trip of such a wide circle. I was still very young in the mid-1800s, and only remember us going further South in the winter, but usually not to the Southwest. The *tatanka* were not as plentiful because the white men hunted them mercilessly.

We kept few possessions and traveled lightly. My grandmothers brought all the *pejuta* with them and harvested more along the way. Other members of the tribe also helped us. The grandmothers knew exactly how to prepare the *pejuta* for traveling. They also brought many sacred spiritual items with them that were very protected and cared for.

The mornings the tribe headed out for a new location were joyous occasions. *Unci* was especially happy when we were preparing to leave an area and travel further. She sang louder and more often than usual. She loved the freedom a new journey brought her and the chance to help other people. She taught me to love it too. I felt especially close to *Wakan Tanka* (Creator) at these times. The *Tatanka Oyate* moved, we the people moved, and all our spirits moved. It was like a beautiful song that the Earth Mother, the sun, the moon, the clouds, the plants, and the animals and people on the land all sung together in harmonious joy. We felt the overwhelming movement of a sacred journey in our hearts and our very beings. We were one together in joyful freedom as we set out in the early dawn of a new day.

There were difficulties at times on our travels. When severe storms came over us, *Unci* taught me not to look at these situations as terrible obstacles. Instead she instructed me to listen to the situation and learn from the teaching it brought. Most rain and snow storms were looked at as blessings from *Wakan Tanka*. We took shelter when a storm approached and prayed together as we thanked *Wakan Tanka* for the blessings of rain and snow and the blessings of protection.

As I grew, I took on more responsibility and tended to much of the *pejuta wakan* (sacred medicines) for my grandmothers, especially when we traveled. Both grandmothers worked with hundreds of people and needed help supplying and caring for the medicines. I was taught to be joyous and peaceful around them. I remained calm and happy in my heart as I worked. No bad feelings or hurtful words were allowed when in the presence of the medicines. I practiced diligently to remain in a state of humility, peace, and love.

There were many rules and responsibilities that our family had to follow in order to do the medicine work. When I wanted to run and play with other children, the grandmothers encouraged me to go and have fun. They often reminded me when I returned from playing that exuberant energy was not allowed around the *pejuta wakan*. Playmates and visitors in general were also not allowed around the medicines. If anyone happened to come too close, the grandmothers quickly smudged the medicines with *pejihota* (sage). All of our family was smudged with *pejihota* each time we tended to the medicines. Our tipi was highly respected by the people, and they knew to keep a respectful distance from the beloved grandmothers who cared for the *pejuta wakan*.

Unci taught me that every living thing had a spirit, a soul, and these souls needed to be respected and honored. She told me souls were in all people, all plants, all animals, and especially in our *Ina Maka* (Earth Mother). Her plants were *waste'* (good) and *wakan* (sacred) with no evil around them. They were pure and needed our protection for the medicine work. The grandmothers did their best to protect the *pejuta wakan* from any negativity coming from humans or any evil that could come to them and infect them. They in turn honored us with their immense healing power and blessings.

Unci believed that there was not an illness on the Earth that couldn't be healed with *pejuta wakan*. She taught me that *Wakan Tanka* had a *pejuta* for all illnesses and it was up to the medicine people to listen to the plants, animals, and spirits to learn what would treat each specific sickness. *Unci* said that some illnesses were in the body, but many were in the mind and in the soul. I was taught to listen and learn the differences in illnesses so that I could pray for the right medicinal plant.

As we traveled to different places, *Unci* often remembered where plants grew in those specific areas. At other times the spirits would tell her something new. One day while on our travels, a little Comanche boy was brought to us who was gravely ill. When we arrived near his village, his parents summoned *Unci*. Grandmother doctored, but he didn't respond to the medicines and the ceremony that she gave him. She continued to pray for him. During the night, she was awakened by one of her spirits who told her of a *pejuta wakan* that would heal the boy. This medicine was native to that area but unknown to her. The spirit told *Unci* to follow a groundhog that would appear to her when she went out on the land. The spirit told her to go very early in the morning.

As dawn's beautiful fingers of golden light spread across the land, *Unci* and I set out to find the groundhog. We walked a long time and we sang and prayed as the sun moved in the sky. Suddenly the groundhog appeared before us. We both stopped in reverence and listened. At first, I wasn't quite sure what I was hearing and then I realized I too was hearing his instructions to *Unci*. He talked to us in spirit tongue as he led us to the plant. He told Grandmother which part of the plant to use, how to prepare it, and how to give it to the boy.

He showed us one specific plant and stayed with us as we dug the plant for its root. First, we laid down the *cansasa* (red willow bark), said a prayer for the plant, and asked if it wanted to help. The plant wanted to help, so we prepared it carefully to take back with us. We sang a sacred song to the groundhog and told him *wopila* (thank you).

We took the *pejuta wakan* back to the village and prepared it. *Unci* prayed to the spirit of the medicine to heal the dying boy. He remained gravely ill even as we gave him the *pejuta* and did the *Inipi* ceremony. *Unci's* faith and belief in the power of the *pejuta* never wavered as she continued the four days of the *Inipi* ceremony. She remained strong and diligent believing with all her heart that this medicine would heal the boy. Others in the tribe became doubtful and fearful. His parents were strained and discouraged. *Unci* worked with them, explaining how important it was for everyone to stay positive and to believe.

On the morning of the fourth day, the boy sat straight up, looked around and in a bewildered way, and asked us all what was wrong. We rejoiced. The *pejuta wakan*, the prayers, and the ceremonies had saved him and brought him back to life.

Later he was able to join a happy, joyous *wopila* ceremony that followed his amazing recovery. Immense gratitude was the only emotion expressed by those in that wonderful ceremony of great thankfulness.

This was the first time I had received instructions from a spirit animal. Later, *Unci* talked to me about it and asked many questions. She explained why seeing in this way was so important to a healer. She asked me if I thought I could accept this gift and not be afraid of it.

"I can, *Unci*," I answered, "but only if you stay with me."

"I will, *Zintkala Zi Win*. I will stay by your side. One day you will be strong enough to go on your own in these ways, but not for a long time. You're safe with your *Unci*."

She told me I would grow up to be a medicine woman just like her. She told me she knew this to be true because I received the groundhog's very *wakan* (sacred) instructions at a very young age.

After the groundhog's appearance, both grandmothers greatly increased their instructions for me. I wasn't just a little grandchild who helped her grandmothers any longer. They began to give me much higher training in the ways of the *Lakota* medicine women.

4

TO BE FREE

Is to praise *Wakan Tanka*

To be free

Is to take a new journey

To be free

Is to walk in humility

To be free

Is to laugh and be joyful

To be free

Is to have faith in Father Sky

To be free

Is to be one with Mother Earth

To be free

Is to be compassionate

To be free

Is to help the people

Oh Creator, I pray to forever be free.

I knew freedom every day of my young life, and it was a beautiful and joyous feeling. Freedom was our *Lakota* way. *Ina Maka* (Mother Earth) was open and wild with Her ways and at the same time gentle and nurturing to us. We knew how to live with Her. We believed the land belonged to *Ina Maka,* and the sky belonged to Father Sky. We humans belonged to *Wakan Tanka*, our Creator, and so did all life including the plants, animals, and birds.

We were very respectful to all living things. We revered Father Sky's *Wakiyan* (Lightning/Thunder Beings) who brought the storms and provided rain for *Ina Maka's* waters. We cherished our animal families. We called them *oyate* (people). We were human people and they were *Tatanka Oyate* (Buffalo People) or *Tahca Oyate* (Deer People) or *Wanbli Oyate* (Eagle People) or *Sunkawakan Oyate* (Horse People). They were the same as we human people and never less.

Our existence on Earth was dependent on others. We lived off the *tatanka* and treasured them, knowing they were very sacred. When we hunted the *tatanka,* we would prepare for the hunt in a respectful way and honor them. We never wasted any parts of any animal. Everything was used because we were so appreciative of the animal's sacrifice. We prayed for its spirit and laid down an offering. Its sacrifice meant that the people could go on living.

Animals and birds appeared to us in spirit form. They helped with our healings, our travels and at times became our protection. We honored them in prayers and ceremonies. They were part of the four winds of our spiritual beliefs. The spirits often showed themselves to us during our vision quests. They warned us of any impending danger. They protected us from evil spirits or negative influences, and they dwelt side by side with us.

We walked free on the land. The animals walked free on the land. The plants were free on the land. We, the Big Brother tribe, were free to travel with the *tatanka* to doctor other tribes and give of ourselves in this way. The animals were free to roam the vast prairies, hills, and mountains, and live as *Wakan Tanka* created them to live. The plants were free to grow and prosper wherever their mighty seeds could take root.

Complete freedom was our way of life and it was an abundant and boundless blessing from *Wakan Tanka*. Living free with wonderful plants and animals was a life of spiritual discipline and gratitude. All living things on Earth were our teachers and were greatly respected for their contributions. We were in balance with each other, with Mother Earth and Father Sky and with *Wakan Tanka*.

I thought about freedom many times over my lifetime. When I was a Grandmother myself, I learned that our *Lakota* way of life was viewed by the *wasicu* as savage and uncivilized. The truth was the opposite. The *wasicu* lived with very little freedom. Every human being was forced to live in divisions of land and could not cross over these divisions. Animals lost their freedom to fences and ownership by humans. Many, like the *tatanka*, were nearly hunted into extinction. The land was plowed for only certain kinds of plants and many medicine species became extinct on the great Creator's lands. The waters were dammed, and they lost their freedom to flow freely. As a result, many species of plants and animals that survived in flowing waters disappeared.

This was what I saw when I was an old woman. Our freedom was gone and would never return. Our people were forced onto little boxes called reservations and our free way of life was no more. The freedom we once had was lost. As an elder, I remembered the time of my youth when we were able to just walk free. All living species moved with us and we moved with them. We sang every day in a beautiful choir of togetherness. We were one with Mother Earth and Father Sky. All manifestations of our visions seemed possible because they were possible. Yet we had our difficulties and combats because evil was always present. We overcame these trials the best way we could. We lived in our spiritual beliefs and passionately praised *Wakan Tanka* in all our actions.

Freedom was the most beautiful and treasured feeling. Freedom to be one with *Wakan Tanka*, *Ptesan Win*, Mother Earth, Father Sky, the plants, the animals, and the birds, was the most precious of all gifts. My heart was filled with gratitude every day of my long life. I thanked the Creator for letting me live the *Lakota* way and for allowing me to experience the soul's true quest to live free with all of *Wakan Tanka's* creations.

CREATOR HELP ME
To be worthy
Of the medicine work
You gave me
A most precious gift
The gift of a seer
Oh, *Wakan Tanka* help me
To see You first
In all things.

My Father was remarried and had four more children before his death. I felt honored to have brothers and sisters. One of my brothers became a valuable helper to me and protected me most of my adult life. Even though I went to live with my Mother's Mother and they stayed with their family, I visited my brothers and sisters often and we played, laughed, and enjoyed each other.

Only one child in a family of medicine people was chosen to follow in the healer's ways and become a medicine man or woman. The choice was carefully and wisely made. Sometimes no one in the healer's family was found, or the special qualities skipped a generation and were seen in a grandchild. Most children who became medicine people were unusual by regular standards, and some could see spirits at very young ages.

We *Lakota* were vastly open to the spirits and our spiritual life. Our entire existence was based on living in harmony with the Creator and all living things. We worked with spirits and had a clear understanding of the other world. We knew there was good and there was bad on the other side, as well as on Earth. We walked the "red road," which was visualized by picturing ourselves walking down a valley. Mountains of evil were on one side and mountains of good on the other. We were trained not to acknowledge the evil side and to walk in balance between the two mountain ranges. *Unci* taught me not to even think of evil or ever speak its name.

Unci showed me from an early age how to work with the good spirits from the other side. I could see and hear them. As a child, I considered them my companions and *Unci* encouraged me to make friends with them. I often felt the presence of these loving ancient spirits who watched over me as I grew in understanding.

We believed there were good and bad spirits and I was taught how to protect myself from the bad spirits. *Unci* instructed me, carefully monitored my progress and gently corrected me when I made mistakes. It was many years before I ever saw the bad. When I did, I knew what to do, despite being startled.

My childhood was not like other children's. I studied and was instructed from a very young age at the feet of *Unci*. I played with many children including my brothers and sisters, but I thrived like a young trainee most of the time. I was raised to believe that the calling of a seer was directly from *Wakan Tanka* and I needed to remain respectful and grateful.

I grew to appreciate and love the ways of my *Unci* and *Unci Oma*. Being a *Lakota* healer and medicine woman was the most wonderful honor and I remained forever grateful throughout my life. The honorable, loving ancient spirits were always with me, bringing me their friendship, comfort, and guidance.

A SLIVER OF moon
Two planets beneath
Rare and beyond time
In its own dimension
My heart sings
To see it in the sky
My mind deepens
To its breathtaking meaning
It lifts my spirit
Up and soaring
As I stare fixedly
At its magnificence
It holds me
In heavenly rapture
Its missives surround me
In circles of light
Understanding permeates
My very soul
And I am one
With its powerful vision.

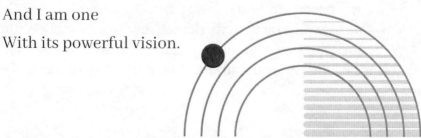

When I first saw the crescent moon with the two planets beneath it, I trembled. I was a young adult at the time and had seen sixteen winters. It was in early December, and a small band of *Lakota* had journeyed with me to *Mato Paha* (Bear Butte Mountain) for my *Hanbleceya* (Vision Quest). *Mato Paha* was located in the Black Hills of South Dakota and was very sacred to the *Lakota*.

Unci had carefully prepared me before we left for *Mato Paha*. She made many special arrangements so that I could *Hanbleceya* during the time of the crescent moon and the two planets. It had been foretold by her spirits that it would be the most optimal time.

I had done an *Hanbleceya* every year for the past three years. I knew the crescent moon and the two planets were not usually part of *Hanbleceya* in the tradition of our people. *Unci* explained it was shown to her that the timing around this event would be the most advantageous for my vision.

Unci organized the small band of people that would travel to *Mato Paha* and leave the tribe behind. They included *Unci, Unci Oma*, two of my brothers, and a special scout sent by our chief who was to watch over us. We were to catch up with the tribe at a designated place and time after my *Hanbleceya*.

It was early December, yet the weather was still warm like the late fall. It was one of those years in the Black Hills when Father Sky held off the snows and freezing temperatures. This too was foretold to *Unci* by her spirits.

We began the *Hanbleceya* with an *Inipi* (Sweat Lodge). We all crawled into a little hut-like structure made from willows and buffalo hides. A fire outside the structure heated the rocks. The hot rocks were brought in and water was poured over them. The resulting steam purified us as we sang sacred songs and smoked the *Canunpa Wakan* (Sacred Pipe).

The *Inipi* would start my four-day and three-night *Hanbleceya*. I would sacrifice food and water all four days while praying on the side of the mountain. *Unci* had timed everything with the coming appearance of the crescent moon and the two planets and the very rare occasion of its presence. We prayed for a successful *Hanbleceya* and a safe trip back to our tribe. Then, we crawled out of the *Inipi*.

I changed from my wet, sweaty clothes into a leather ceremonial dress. I put on a pair of high-legged, fringed moccasins. My grandmothers had beaded the crescent moon and the two planets onto the dress. They put a large buffalo hide around my shoulders for warmth. The crescent moon and the two planets had been carefully painted inside the buffalo hide.

We walked up the side of the sacred mountain to a special place which had been selected for my *Hanbleceya*. The Grandmothers put a second large buffalo hide on the ground and covered it with sage. They helped me situate four red willow branches and put them into the ground around me to form a square. *Unci* guided me inside the square. I had already made four hundred *canli wapahta* (tobacco prayer ties) in preparation for the *Hanbleceya,* and I began to string them around the four branches. I tied the black prayer ties between the two branches that faced West, the red prayer ties were strung between the two branches that faced North, the yellow prayer ties were strung between the next two branches that faced East, and the white prayer ties faced South.

The prayer ties were made with leather or cloth, and tobacco or red willow bark was placed inside each one of them. They were tied together with thin strips of leather. *Unci* had been able to trade for cloth in the four colors from the white traders. She liked the idea of reflecting the actual colors of the four directions during the special time of an *Hanbleceya*.

We believed we were spiritually protected inside the square formed by the branches and prayer ties, and as a result, nothing bad or negative could penetrate. I put small red willow sticks in the ground to hold my *Canunpa Wakan* and sat down on the bed of buffalo hide and sage. I prepared myself to stay within the area of the branches and prayer ties for four days. My grandmothers blessed me and would keep the fire going down the hill at the sweat lodge during my *Hanbleceya*. *Unci* told me she would climb up and check on me from time to time. I was to pray for a vision during these very special four days and three nights.

I knew it was much harder to *Hanbleceya* during the early winter. Most people did their prayers for a vision when the weather was warm. *Unci* had carefully instructed me on why it was so important to pray and ask for a vision during the very rare time of the alignment of the crescent moon and the two planets. She told me that it was a special time because it was an unparalleled opening to the spirit world and that she had been told to have me *Hanbleceya* at this time.

After I was situated, everyone quietly left me and went to the bottom of the hill to tend to the fire. I lifted my *Canunpa Wakan* to the West, then the North, the East and the South. I lifted my *Canunpa Wakan* up to Father Sky and down to Mother Earth. I continued to hold the sacred pipe as I prayed for a vision. I watched the sun streak rays of sunshine across the land and surround the mountain. I continued to pray.

I sat all the first day and prayed with my *Canunpa Wakan*. Sometimes I kept my eyes closed and other times I opened them. And still I prayed. I saw white fluffy clouds float overhead, birds busily searching for food, and a curious deer. I heard the cries of several *wanbli* and knew many lived on the mountain.

It was a beautiful early winter day and still quite warm. The sun poured its energy on me and I was grateful. At times, the white clouds formed shapes in the sky and sent me messages. They were so wonderful. I felt very happy and honored to be sitting with *Mato Paha*.

I watched as the sun lazily moved across the sky towards the evening shadows of the West. I remained in prayer holding my *Canunpa Wakan*. As the sun started to set, noises of the birds and little animals gradually faded away. I reached for the buffalo robe and put it around my shoulders. The shadows of dusk floated across the land in a peaceful play of light and dark.

I glanced up at the Southwestern sky and saw the first sight of the crescent moon with the two planets. The alignment seemed to leap out at me. I stared and stared at the sight as my eyes became transfixed in amazement. The crescent shape of the moon faced upwards with the left point slightly lower than the right. Two very bright planets lined up directly below the crescent shape. The alignment was brighter than anything around it. I knew instantly that this was the special sighting *Unci* had prepared me for. It took my breath away, and I sat there in a state of wonder.

After a time, I realized I had become mesmerized by the crescent moon and the two planets. It held me spellbound and fascinated. I could not avert my eyes. I stared and stared as I sat riveted on my buffalo hide holding my *Canunpa Wakan*. The crescent moon and the two planets held my intense gaze for what seemed like a long time.

Suddenly I realized the alignment was communicating with me. Flashes of visions rapidly rushed over me. It was so fast and powerful I wondered at times if I could even remain sitting up. My body trembled and shook while my human mind was sent into the background. I saw the visions deeply in my soul. They permeated my very being and it felt like I became one with them.

The crescent moon and the two planets sent me vivid predictions so rapidly I could hardly take breaths. Revelations poured over me and I saw wondrous lights and thousands of voices singing all at the same time. I sat frozen in astonishment and awe at all the phenomena I witnessed.

At some point, I realized hours and hours had passed without me being aware of time or where I was. The crescent moon and the two planets had sent me vision after vision, minute by minute, and hour after hour.

The visions finally reached an ending and I closed my eyes and said prayers of profound gratitude. I felt such deep reverence for all that I had been shown. I prayed over and over in complete thankfulness to *Wakan Tanka* and held myself in the brilliance and wonderment of what had just occurred.

7

FLASHES OF LIGHT

Roll across the land

The *Wakiyan*

Thunder their arrival

They appear nearer

I see them

In all four directions

Their lightning brilliant

Their thunder deafening

They approach me

I quietly tremble

In shaken silence

My reverence for them

Immense and immeasurable

They dance around me

Wondrous and free

And I join them

In unending blessedness.

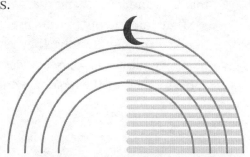

I saw the *Wakiyan* (Lightning and Thunder Beings) suddenly appear and quickly move across the land. It was surprising to see them without any clouds, just their energetic flashes. The alignment of the crescent moon and the two planets was still bright in the sky. The lightning came closer and closer and for a time lit up around the crescent moon and the two planets. They danced together in a brilliant show of oneness as the lightning joined the alignment and became one with it.

I realized I was having a vision. The *Wakiyan* moved quickly, appeared right before me, then lifted me above my buffalo hide. My spirit soared and met the lightning beings up in the sky as they carefully instructed me.

"We are powerful spirits," they began. "We don't always have to dance on the Earth. Some day we may stop and then the Earth will suffer. As time goes forward humans will appreciate us less and less. They won't understand that we ignite life itself. Without us, all will die."

They communicated with me in a loving, kind way and I immediately understood the knowledge they were trying to give me.

"In the future, most humans will not thank us. We don't have to come every spring and wake up *Ina Maka* (Mother Earth) so that all can grow. We do it because we love the Mother and we want the best for Her and all who live on Her. Your people do thank us and love us and that's why we honor them."

They told me my prayers for a vision were being granted. I thanked them gratefully. They revealed they were the helpers of an overall vision, one that was long and intense and would come to me over the next days and nights of my *Hanbleceya*.

They informed me that I would remember this vision for my entire life, and possibly into my other lifetimes.

"*Wopila, wopila* (thank you, thank you)," I whispered over and over.

The *Wakiyan* continued to proclaim, "There will be spiritual storms of great magnitude coming. The storms will manifest physically, but they will also be energetic. *Wakan Tanka* will send a physical washing, an energetic washing, and a spiritual washing. He will raise the spiritual energy as wondrous gateways from the Heavens open for the future of our Earth Mother."

They instructed me that the vision had been put into me as they talked and as I continued to watch the crescent moon and the two planets. They told me I would see all of the vision during the days and nights of my *Hanbleceya*. They informed me that the rare alignment of the crescent moon and the two planets had closed and that its extraordinary opening to the spirit world was only for one night.

The *Wakiyan* gently sat me back down on the buffalo hide surrounded by my prayer ties. They said they would stay with me the next days and nights of my *Hanbleceya* and help me to fully see the rest of the vision. I thanked them over and over. They said they appreciated my gratitude. They expressed that being thankful and grateful was a very powerful medicine and to always stay in an intense state of gratitude.

8

OH CREATOR

I am young
And my eyes see
Into the future
Of a coming time
I do not
Want to see
Help me Creator
Understand Your
Divine purpose.

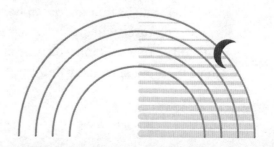

I held my *Canunpa Wakan* tightly in prayer. It was a clear night on the mountain and very quiet. I was peaceful and grateful.

I felt my heart speed up and my muscles tighten when I heard the thunder crash and saw the lightning fire to the ground. Fear came into my mind because of the sudden sounds. In the next instant, the *Wakiyan* lifted me up into the sky. They quickly extinguished my fear. I was one with them as they instructed me to focus on what they would show me in the next part of the vision.

They told me of a coming time when *Wakan Tanka* would raise the Earth to a new spiritual level.

"Every living human, animal, and plant on Earth will be touched," they said.

"The Earth Mother herself will be touched, including Her sacred rocks, soil, and even Her inner fire. *Wakan Tanka* will show His power to all good on the Earth and to all evil. Nothing on the Earth will avoid *Wakan Tanka* during the time that is to come.

"*Wakan Tanka* will command a spiritual cleansing of the entire Earth Planet. It will come as immense rain from the skies and waves from the oceans. He will lead a complete washing of spiritual energy and cause gateways to open from beyond the stars. Many of the Benevolent Ones, who once walked on Earth, will return through special openings. They will help all creation on Earth.

"There will be momentous upheaval during the coming time. Many creatures will suffer. Many will survive but with great difficulty. Some will find the time of great cleansing and change to be hard but spiritually uplifting.

"There will be much destruction on Earth as *Wakan Tanka* eliminates that which no longer needs to exist. The powerful energy which He is sending will cause immense upheaval. Volcanoes will erupt. The Earth will slide and move. The seas will shift. Great storms will charge across the prairies. Dry crusted lands will appear where none were before. These days will be hard.

"When the coming time finally arrives, enormous damage will have been done to our Earth Mother by humans and by evil. *Wakan Tanka* will see the devastation done to the planet and be very saddened. The intense damage done to Mother Earth will make Her very sick. She will be in a damaged state as She tries to move into a new era that *Wakan Tanka* has already created for Her and which is to be manifested in the future. This transition will be much more difficult for *Ina Maka* as a result of Her sickness and suffering, and much more difficult for all who live on Her. That is why *Wakan Tanka* will walk the Earth in the coming time so that He can restore Her health and heal Her."

Still clutching my *Canunpa Wakan* and listening to the *Wakiyan* as they showed me the coming time of *Wakan Tanka*, I became afraid. I instantly thought of my grandmothers, my brothers and sisters, my people and what could happen to them. I wondered what part humans could possibly play in making *Ina Maka* so sick. We *Lakota* walked in harmony with the land and all of *Wakan Tanka's* creations. I felt sad and I wanted to weep.

The *Wakiyan* quickly showered me in a beautiful blue mist and gave me the gift of a brave heart. I realized their gift as it swept over me and I thanked them gratefully. A new realization came with the blue mist. The vision of a coming time was all in *Wakan Tanka's* plan and there would also be a way for us to survive.

"*Zintkala Zi Win*," they called to me. "You are to be a leader of your people. With our blessing, we bestow upon you the medicine from the West where we *Wakiyan* live and where the storms originate. Your *Unci* has helped you become a young medicine woman. You are also blessed with the seeing medicine. We will be with you and help you lead the people."

"*Wopila, wopila,*" I replied. I felt very grateful for their love, concern, and instruction. I knew the vision I received was very important and I thanked them from my heart for showing it to me.

The *Wakiyan* continued the vision of the coming time by showing me blessings that were also to appear.

"*Wakan Tanka* will need to destroy evil and all entities that can no longer exist, but He will also bring new energy which will be very powerful and full of love and peace. *Wakan Tanka's* new energy will be essential to help Mother Earth sustain Her life and all the life that She supports. In order for Her to go on and be plentiful once again, there will need to be a very dramatic shift from where she will be in the coming time. The new energy will usher in waves of powerful love that will encircle the Earth."

I was filled with hope and understanding. Gently, the *Wakiyan* placed me back down on the buffalo hide surrounded by my prayer ties.

"There is much more for you to see and learn," they instructed. "Close your eyes for a while and ponder all that you have seen. We will continue the vision a little later."

I closed my eyes and felt an immediate rush of love flow over me. My heart wanted to sing, and my mind wanted to applaud the wonder of the *Wakiyan*. I became enveloped in their glorious peace of understanding.

OH, MIGHTY EAGLE

I hear you
Floating with
The night sky
High above the
Majestic mountain
You glide peacefully
Above me
My soul wants
To soar with you
To look down
And see what you see
To be free
And fly above
All things below
Wanbli Gleska
Take me with you
That my spirit too
May forever fly free.

I was very grateful to be on the hillside of *Mato Paha* at this early winter time. Everything was unusually quiet around me in the stillness of the night. The breezes were gentle, the air was crisp, and all was tranquil. I smiled and felt especially blessed and happy.

I first heard the *Wanbli Gleska* (Spotted Eagle) before I saw him. His eagle cry pierced the air and made every living thing rise to attention. I looked in his direction. He quickly flew toward me and circled me four times. My soul rose wanting to join the revered Eagle. Suddenly he landed right in front of me and began giving me messages. It was the next part of my vision.

"Your *oyate* (people) will go to a high place," he advised. "Many *wamakaskan* (animals) will go to high places where all shall weather the coming storms and be safe. Many *oyate* will hear the call to go to high places across the Earth. Those that heed the call will be spared. Those that do not heed the call will not be spared. It will be the will of *Wakan Tanka*. It will be the faith of humans that leads them to the high places.

"The *wamakaskan* (animals), *zintkala* (birds) and *wabluska* (insects) will know long before humans hear the calling to move. You will see massive migrations of birds to special places and you will see significant gatherings of animals. *Wakan Tanka* will provide many places of safety across *Ina Maka*.

"Watch the different migratory patterns of *zintkala*. Their migrations will be a sign and a signal of the coming time. Watch the *kimimila* (butterflies), especially the monarchs. In the coming time, you will see more of them around you and they will tell you when the changes begin to happen. The *wanbli* (eagles) will circle you, speak to you and sing to you. Listen very carefully.

"*Zintkala Zi Win*, when the time is near, other people will notice spirit *kimimila* around you, especially the children. Some *wamakaskan* and *oyate* will sometimes see spirit *wanbli* fly above you. Listen to these reports from others as they are signs to you.

"The *Wakiyan* will make their presence known and be around you especially during storms. Even in winter they can come for you and dance with you. Listen to them carefully.

"As the times get more difficult for all living things on the Earth Planet, you must remember that *Wakan Tanka's* great cleansing is necessary because *Ina Maka* will become sicker and sicker. You will help others understand about Her illness, why it's happening, and bring hope to them.

"In the coming time as *Ina Maka* becomes increasingly ill, the *wasicu* will invent a terrible and exceedingly destructive weapon to fight wars. They will not fully realize that the weapon will destroy the very essence of creation and eventually cause total earthly destruction. They will falsely believe they can control it.

"The new weapon will utilize vibrations. It will be used to cause large scale ruin or the death of a single person. It will have the ability to do either massive annihilation or small isolated destruction. Such flexibility will be its appeal.

"No people or species on land or in the waters will be able to hear the weapon as it approaches. They will be able to feel massive earthquake-like waves of vibration minutes before it hits. It will turn everything it touches into dust. The vibration weapon won't just destroy—it will interfere with the very core of all living things. It will cause damage to *Wakan Tanka's* creations and the world He created.

"Because all life has a vibrational beginning and the new weapon will destroy using vibration, it will be the worst kind of weapon. It will cause immense changes to the vibrational whole which makes up the universe of *Wakan Tanka*. His planet, His people, His animals and all His creations will be altered and changed for the worse. The vibration weapon must never be invented or used.

"*Wakan Tanka* will not allow changes or threats to the very matter of creation. He will walk the Earth during the coming time, destroy that which needs to be destroyed and aid humans to start over. He will help them learn to use the vibration of love to rule their hearts and not the vibration of destruction.

"*Wakan Tanka* loves *Ina Maka* and all who live on Her. He doesn't see humans as negative or evil. All are born on *Ina Maka* and into *waste'* (good) but some humans allow themselves to be taken over by evil. It makes *Wakan Tanka* very sad and He yearns for them to learn and return to the good.

"The many changes *Ina Maka* will endure during the coming time have never been seen before. As the time approaches, the changes won't immediately be recognized. You, *Zintkala Zi Win*, will be given signs to see and follow. There will be warnings from the *kimimila*, the *wanbli*, and the *wakiyan*. Others will also come to warn you. These will all be signs for you to see so that you can help others. As you live your life, you will often wonder when your vision will come into reality. Look and listen very carefully for the signs. That will be the beginning."

I felt nausea in my stomach as the *Wanbli Gleska* finished telling me of the coming time. I wanted to cry and yell out that it couldn't possibly happen. "Not that way," my human mind cried out, trying to reject what I had just been shown.

The *Wanbli Gleska* watched me. He didn't move as he saw how I struggled.

"You are a young person," he began. "It would be abnormal for you not to have feelings right now because you care deeply for others. The part of the vision I just showed you is difficult to see. But remember: a medicine woman does not have time for doubt or worry. Keep your belief and your faith in *Wakan Tanka* very strong so that He can work through you in the coming time."

I realized he was trying to help and I immediately replied, "I give you my word. I will stay strong as my *Unci* has taught. *Wopila. Wopila* for all that you have shown me. *Wopila.*"

The *Wanbli Gleska* flapped his wings as his vision instructions ended, and then lifted himself upwards. He soared around me four times and then flew higher and higher to the Heavens. I could only hear him calling out into the night.

"*Wopila, wopila*," I cried out to him again and again as he glided away.

10

FEAR, I SUFFER you
Worry, I know you
My body responds
And wants to flee
My mind races
And goes in circles
Then the teachings
Come back to me
When the fear rises
I go into my heart
And be thankful
I keep my heart
In gratitude
I remember
Nothing negative
Can conquer
A grateful heart.

I saw the flashes of lightning and heard the loud rolls of thunder as the *Wakiyan* leapt across the night sky.

Before I knew what was happening, I was up in the sky with them as they showed me the next part of the vision. Together we rode as we watched the land below fly by, mirroring large shadows of clouds. I soared and flew with them as vast expanses of land raised themselves in greeting. I felt like I was on a giant pony riding gallantly and swiftly across the sky. I knew a freedom I had never before experienced, and I was in utter happiness.

I glanced to the far horizon as we approached it and saw balls of fire in the distance and heard large roaring sounds. I was startled and became fearful. We were flying right into the disturbances. My mind told me to stop and go back but there was no turning around.

The *Wakiyan* quickly spoke to me.

"You are seeing and hearing the coming time of the great vibrational cleansing from *Wakan Tanka*," the *Wakiyan* directed as they held my attention. "We are showing you a vision. Do not be afraid. In the coming time, *Ina Maka* will first be cleansed with storms of water. The storms will be followed with a cleansing consisting of vast waves of sound and fire. The cleansing sound will come from massive vibrations and it will be very frightening. The cleansing fire ball will come from an intense infinite light and it will be especially unusual and cause panic.

"For all species on Earth who have loved *Wakan Tanka* and have been led to His special places, precautions and preparations will have been made. When the great vibrational cleansing descends with heavenly sounds and lights they will know how to survive it.

"To some, *Wakan Tanka's* great cleansing of sound and light will be a wide and beautiful blessing. To others it will be a vast destruction never before seen or heard on Earth. After the cleansing, great peace and love will be restored to *Ina Maka*. *Wakan Tanka* is a loving Creator who will cleanse *Ina Maka* in the coming time and provide for all His creation.

"*Zintkala Zi Win*, you will be told how to be protected and how to survive the great vibrational cleansing. You will keep seeing the future of this and you will prepare yourself and others. Let not your mind ask questions for now. All will be answered in time."

"*Wopila, wopila*," I muttered in awe and reverence.

The *Wakiyan* landed me gently back on my buffalo hide surrounded by my prayer ties. I was honored by their instructions and extremely humbled. I wondered about this part of the vision with such life-and-death instructions. I knew not to question anything I was shown. I picked up my *Canunpa Wakan* from the pipe stand and closed my eyes to pray. I surrendered my heart to complete and engulfing gratitude.

11

MIGHTY *TATANKA*

I feel your hooves

Running across

The lush land

Spurring vibrations

Of great strength

And endless courage

Run, run

Oh *Tatanka*

Run for your

Existence

Run away

Save yourselves

You are *wakan*

Powerful and pure

Run *Tatanka*

Run away

Into the forever.

It was very dark and still the first night of my prayers for a vision. I realized it could be day or night in the visions, but when not in vision it was actual day and night like usual on Earth.

A large pounding sound startled me and interrupted my thoughts. It became louder and louder as I wondered what was happening. After listening for a few minutes, I realized in astonishment the sounds were the running hooves of *Tatanka Oyate* (Buffalo People). The pounding sounds became so great that I thought the *tatanka* herd must stretch for miles and miles in every direction. I could see dust rise in the distance from their running. My heart beat faster and I felt the ground shake as if to welcome them into spellbound attention.

My entire body shook as I listened to the pounding of the *tatanka* hooves. I couldn't really see them off in the distance but everything around me could feel their presence. We *Lakota* relied on *tatanka*. We were one with *tatanka*. We depended on *tatanka* for food, warmth and inspiration. When a buffalo gave his life for us we were grateful, and we said prayers for him. *Tatanka* rewarded our reverence by giving us vast spiritual knowledge and essential healings chiefly of strength and courage.

My mind and body were held in rapt attunement as I listened to the *tatanka* run in the distance. Just as the ground around me vibrated at a high level and I wondered if the buffalo would run my way, I saw a lone *Tatanka* appear and walk slowly toward me. She ambled carefully from the North. She approached me cautiously and I realized she didn't want to alarm me. As she walked right up in front of me and stopped, I knew not to be afraid because I realized I was being shown a vision. She was now very close to me and I held my breath in anticipation of what her visit might mean. She deliberately snorted her buffalo sounds several times. As her noises landed on my ears I realized she was sending me messages. They flooded my mind and soul.

She showed me images of many *tatanka* gatherings. The pictures came to me quickly and I saw buffalo herds that were so magnificent that it looked like they would envelop the Earth. She told me that in the coming time of the great cleansing, the *tatanka* will once again run across the prairies in large herds and their numbers will be vast and impressive.

Her warning followed. I heard the prophecy, but she didn't show it to me in pictures, sparing me from possible endless grief. She told me there will be a time on Earth when *tatanka* will almost cease to exist and be no more. Strangers from other lands will kill the revered *tatanka* into near extinction, she foretold. Anger welled from deep within my belly. I wanted to shout out in disbelief. I couldn't imagine a time when there would be so few *tatanka* or how so many could be killed. It didn't seem possible.

I felt a calm fall over me as the *Tatanka* spoke and reassured me. "In the coming time, when *Wakan Tanka* returns, the *tatanka* herds will gather again and run freely across the land. Old ones will sacrifice themselves so that your people can have meat and warmth from their hides. *Zintkala Zi Win*, always remember the ways of the *tatanka*, their medicines, their ceremonies and the ways of survival for your people with the *tatanka*. Keep these ways in your heart. In the coming time, return to being the big brothers and big sisters of the *Lakota* so that you can help other people.

"Whenever a *Tatanka Ska* (White Buffalo) appears, bow down to her. She is very sacred, and when she appears there is always an important prophetic message. Whether you see a *Tatanka Ska* in spirit or see one alive, bow down and receive her special instructions. She is very rare."

I was reminded that the *Canunpa Wakan* I was holding and praying with was brought by *Ptesan Win* (White Buffalo

Calf Woman). She brought the *Canunpa Wakan* so the people could make their prayers in a very sacred way while using the holy pipe. *Ptesan Win* also gave the *Lakota* people seven sacred ceremonies to follow. They included the *Inipi* (Sweat Lodge), the *Hanbleceya* (Vision Quest) and the *Wiwanyang Wacipi* (Sun Dance).

The *Tatanka* continued instructing me. "When *Ptesan Win* appears, you will know something of great importance will be told to you or will be brought forth. As the coming time approaches, you will begin to see Her. She will personally instruct you on survival, prayer, ceremonies, and healings. She will lead you as the time comes closer. She will ask you to share this knowledge with others, so they too will know what to do. Follow her directions carefully.

"There will be Benevolent Ones in other lands who will come by way of visions and sightings to help their people during the coming time. Know and remember that *Wakan Tanka* will take care of all the different kinds of peoples living on *Ina Maka*.

"Evil ones will also appear, and many people will follow them. They will make themselves seem to be stronger. They will use words that look as if they are true in an attempt to ward off the coming time when *Wakan Tanka* walks the Earth again. Masses of people will be deceived.

"The evil ones will disguise themselves. Many people will be fooled. *Zintkala Zi Win*, you need to be very careful. Always check the energy around people. Really look. The malevolent individuals cannot maintain any semblance of good energy for a long period of time. An evil person cannot hold the beautiful energy of love and compassion if it isn't there to begin with. The energy around them is actually jagged or too many colors are around them or dirty or dim colors. You will feel and know something is not right. Pay careful attention.

"Be vigilant. Evil will never let you see what it really looks like as it walks around in everyday life disguised in people or places. Wicked people also learn to use evil spirits from the other side.

Sometimes outward behavior of certain people clearly indicates that evil is present, but often evil is very clever at hiding. Check the energy. Check the behavior. Even a little shadow of doubt that comes into your mind is a warning sign. You will need to be very careful because evil knows of the coming time and will fight more strongly than ever before.

"Be hopeful. You will survive. *Wakan Tanka* is love and purity and goodness and humor and peace. *Ina Maka* will be beautiful again and restored to complete health after the cleansing of the coming time has been completed. Keep all that I have shown you in your heart and soul. Never question when the coming time might happen. Only *Wakan Tanka* knows. It could be in another lifetime for you. No one knows but Him. Pray deeply with your *Canunpa Wakan* on all that you have been shown. Put these messages from the Creator so deeply in your soul that it can be awakened in a time for you that is yet to come."

"*Wopila, wopila,*" I gratefully replied to the majestic *Tatanka* standing before me. "I am very humbled for the vision and instructions you have given me. I will listen and follow and put everything you have told me deep into my heart."

The *Tatanka* held my gaze for a long time as if to further emblazon her visions into my soul. She slowly and deliberately turned back around to the North as she walked away. I thought about all she had told me. I clutched my *Canunpa Wakan* and prayed that all the *tatanka* would be spared in the coming time when it was prophesied their numbers would dwindle.

FEATHER WHISPERS

Gently fill my ears

Masses of eagles

Come into view

From the skies

Glowing white lights

Appear among

The circling eagles

I hold my breath

Stunned and silenced

By the beauty

Human forms

Materialize

In the whiteness

I see they are

Spirits of another time

The Benevolent Ones

Come back

To help the people.

My heart felt heavy after watching the *Tatanka* walk away. She was majestic and beautiful and wise. I could not imagine people who did not honor all the *tatanka* the way our people did. I remembered *Unci's* instructions about visions and how during an *Hanbleceya* they were especially important and always with special meaning. Her thoughts gave me comfort and hope.

I held my *Canunpa Wakan* in prayer. It would soon be the first night of my prayers for a vision. I saw the dark clouds before I noticed the *Wakiyan* flashing their arrival. They quickly moved to the hill I was sitting on. I instantly knew they were bringing another part of the vision. I felt myself lifted up into the sky with them as we travelled across the land together.

The *Wakiyan* showed me majestic beings descending down from the skies toward Earth. They were far off, but I could see beautiful white all around them. I looked down at the land and realized it was shaking and the waves on the waters were standing high to greet the beautiful beings. It was *Ina Maka* rejoicing to see them. They were arriving to help Her, and I could see She was happy.

"*Wakan Tanka* will send his Benevolent Spirits from the skies to help in the coming time," explained the *Wakiyan*. "Some once walked the Earth as *Tunkasila* (Grandfather Spirits) and *Unci Makata* (Grandmother Spirits) in every land, and spiritually led and helped their people. *Ptesan Win* will direct them as they approach the planet's atmosphere. They will be escorted onto the Earth realm by masses of *Wanbli Gleska* (Spotted Eagles) who will help guide them with their incredible vision. The Benevolent Spirits will descend quietly between the whisperings of *wanbli* wings and they will be bathed in stunning white light.

"They will come to establish a new earthly order. The Benevolent Spirits will lead humans to different societies of peace and love. Life on *Ina Maka* (Mother Earth) will steadily improve until completely changed over to the *waste'* (good).

"In time as the Benevolent Spirits work with the people, there will be no war. Human hearts will be filled with peace, love, and compassion. Earth will be a place of great learning, and souls will be better able to transform themselves, so they can progress much further after leaving the Earth plane.

"The transformation of *Ina Maka* will take many years. It will be the ushering in of a new era that *Wakan Tanka* willed, prophesized, and determined. He did not envision that humankind would alter the health of *Ina Maka*. She will be very sick in the coming time. As a result, and as the new era tries to materialize, the transformation of *Ina Maka* will be far more difficult than it would have been if human greed, human apathy, and evil entities had never been allowed to grow into the serious strength they will possess.

"The Benevolent Spirits will be kind, patient, and loving, and will set up beautiful places for education. As a result, all humans in various stages of learning will be able to grow and mature their souls. *Ina Maka* will become a higher spiritual school, and humans will be eager to learn and become advanced spiritual beings. The planet will become the great example of *Wakan Tanka's* love to advance souls in His own likeness.

"Earth will not be perfect. Humans will still have free will. The Benevolent Spirits will establish a new justice system to help humans make better choices and to lovingly correct their paths in life for the highest maturing of their souls.

"Earth will be a more blessed, loving, and spiritual place to learn. *Ina Maka* will be beautiful and restored to Her original splendor. All life will feel considerable gratitude to be able to live on Earth. The Benevolent Spirits will help the people advance in all areas of their lives. They will stay for several years. They will eventually leave when humans can go forward again on their own.

"The Benevolent Spirits will come to every land and all people across the planet of *Ina Maka*. They will be recognized by people in every religion. They will be welcomed by the good and rejected by the bad.

"*Zintkala Zi Win,* when the *Wanbli Gleska* congregate in great numbers you will know the Benevolent Spirits are getting ready to arrive. Be prepared. Their numbers will be so big that the sound of *wanbli* wings descending from the skies will be like masses and masses of whispering feathers against joyous currents of air."

My ears heard the whispering of feathers and saw the *Wanbli Gleska* descending in a clockwise pattern as they slowly entered Earth's atmosphere and descended into the blue skies of *Ina Maka*. My mind soared to see them, and I wanted to fly and be with their powerful presence.

I found myself back on my buffalo hide and surrounded by my prayer ties.

"Rest a while," I heard the *Wakiyan* say. "The next part of your vision will be hard for you to view."

"*Wopila, wopila,*" I replied gratefully.

The *Wakiyan* disappeared into the clouds as quickly as they had appeared. I let the vision of the new beautiful times on *Ina Maka* fill my mind as I gently closed my eyes for a few moments. I prayed in deep gratitude for the vision of earthly love and peace I had just been shown.

13

NO WORDS

Must ever

Describe

Evil

No ears

Ought ever

Hear it

No eyes

Need even

See it

No mind

Should ever

Think it

So crushing

Is its

Power

To call us

To it.

It was the middle of the night when the *Wakiyan* returned to show me the next part of the vision. They gently lifted me up into the sky with them. We flew swiftly across the prairies. It seemed like we flew a very long time. The *Wakiyan* slowed their pace and danced in place. I heard ghastly sounds. As we approached the sounds, a large threatening fireball came into view.

Before I could see too much, the *Wakiyan* quickly spoke to me.

"*Ina Maka* will tremble violently and open with monstrous pits all across the planet just like the one you see off in the distance. All evil ones, demons, and evil humans will be pushed and will fall into the large pits. The pits will be highly explosive and will shake and erupt like gigantic earthquakes and volcanoes. Evil will have absolutely no way of escaping.

"*Wakan Tanka* will send giant fireballs of destructive energy into the pits. The evil will be destroyed instantly. It will be reduced to ashes in seconds. There will be no remains. There will be no souls left. There will be nothing left. Evil will be dead forever from the fireballs of vast destructive energy."

We flew a little closer to the monstrous pit. I heard horrible screams and ghastly yells beyond anything I had ever before heard. I saw human bodies fly shrieking into the pits followed by demons in many disgusting forms. Millions and millions of people flew into the pits. There were so many that my eyes had trouble accepting what I saw. Every form that was pushed into the pit by an unseen force was in horrid agony. The sound of the pit was deafening. The smell was putrid beyond explanation. The sight of the pit, even from a safe distance, was horrifying.

I felt my distressed stomach want to give. Disgust filled every part of me and I heaved into the night air. The vast pit was repulsive and hideous, and I needed to turn away. I prayed to *Wakan Tanka* to give me courage and help me understand the need to see the horror. I quickly reminded myself that all visions during an *Hanbleceya* are sacred and for a purpose.

"*Ina Maka* will later close herself around the pit and the remaining ashes," the *Wakiyan* continued to show me. "She will swallow the ashes and take them to Her core of fire, where they will be reduced to nothingness. Evil shall never exist again. The evil that was on Earth will be gone forever. At no time in the future will humans be infected by evil or tempted by evil.

"The new coming era and way of being will be led by the Benevolent Spirits across the world and will be one of goodness, peace, and love. Humans will still make wrong choices due to free will. When they do, the Benevolent Spirits will help them correct their thoughts and actions, so they can mature to a more loving generous nature.

"Never again will *Wakan Tanka* allow a wrong choice by a human to cause Him to be overtaken by evil. Never again will *Wakan Tanka* allow evil to take over a human and then use that soul for the bad and against others. In the coming time, all humans will be allowed to progress on their path of love, kindness, generosity, peace, and compassion."

The *Wakiyan* turned around and we flew back to the hill of my *Hanbleceya*. They gently guided me to my buffalo hide surrounded by my prayer ties.

"Do not dwell on what we have shown you. Take it out of your mind immediately. You were shown this vision so you would know beyond all doubt how evil will be destroyed and taken from the Earth. You will help others with their doubts. After seeing this vision, there is no way you would ever question the wisdom of *Wakan Tanka* or His ability to rule over evil. He will not let His creation be destroyed.

"His ways are like the blink of an eye compared to time as is seen on Earth. Do not question when or why as your *Unci* has always instructed you. Restore your mind now in prayer and remain in deep faith to the Creator. Close your eyes for a time. Concentrate and pray on the good that is coming."

"*Wopila, wopila,*" I called after them as they lingered for a moment. "I will do all that you have asked. I will not dwell on this part of the vision."

"*Waste', waste',*" they answered as they disappeared into clouds that quickly caught the winds and vanished.

14

WE WALK
Together
With Father Sky
And Mother Earth
Every living soul
Has its balance
With the whole
As we connect
With the Other
Oh Creator
Help me stay
In balance
Within my being
And with all
Your creation.

While praying with my *Canunpa Wakan*, I rested my mind. The mountain remained in the darkness of my first night.

I heard the thunder and opened my eyes to see the *Wakiyan* move across the sky. I remained seated on my buffalo hide and surrounded by my prayer ties.

For this part of the vision, the *Wakiyan* did not have me fly with them. Instead, they quickly sent me visions, which poured into my very soul as I remained on the mountain. They showed me a time before *Wakan Tanka* would walk the Earth, when *Ina Maka* would become seriously ill. She will keep praying and praying for *Wakan Tanka* to come help Her. As Her sickness spreads, She will desperately try to heal Herself by restoring Her balance. As She frantically fights for survival, there will be incredible extremes across the planet.

There will be more hot and more cold temperatures. The storms will rage in severity, or there will be no storms. The rain will pour waters of unending torrents, or there will be complete drought. Bitter cold temperatures will be present in winter, followed by extremely hot temperatures in summer.

There will be more lightning, causing more fires. There will be more lightning strikes as the *Wakiyan* try to bring *Ina Maka* out of Her sickness by jolting Her heart back to beating. In some places, there will be no lightning, as the *Wakiyan* decide to retreat in utter disgust. Overall there will be millions more electric charges worldwide created by lightning and never seen by humans.

There will be plentiful food, or there will be worldwide starvation. Increasingly, people will see failed crops, food shortages, and famine. The stockpiling of food will become very necessary as Mother Earth's production of crops becomes less predictable.

There will be massive windstorms and tornadoes, or there will be no movement of air at all as the planet fights for Her balance. The rivers will overrun their banks violently, or have so little water flowing that it will putrefy. Fires will rage wildly out of control, or fire itself will be snuffed into near nothingness.

The *Wakiyan* showed me a time before *Wakan Tanka's* return, when *Ina Maka* will be in terrible sickness and peril. I saw that humans and evil would be responsible for the harm done to Her. I was stunned by what I saw because our *Lakota* people had always considered the cause and effect of all actions for seven generations past us. I knew that even the animals recognized the need to live free with *Ina Maka* and not do harm to their own home.

I saw that humans will know that they are harming *Ina Maka* in the coming time. They will have the wisdom and knowledge to know what they are doing. They won't be innocent as if they were in a different and unknowing time. They will know in every way not to harm the Earth Mother. They will know, and they will harm Her anyway.

I continued sitting in the darkness and clutching my *Canunpa Wakan*. I felt complete hopelessness. We *Lakota* had the highest love for *Ina Maka*. I wondered who the humans were that cared so little. I pondered that they must be very hardened of heart and exceedingly cruel. I realized in that moment that they were part of the evil that *Wakan Tanka* would confront in the coming time when He walked again on the Earth.

The *Wakiyan* spoke. "The vision of the suffering of *Ina Maka* in the coming time is very difficult to see. We know you love Her and want to take good care of Her, as do your people. This vision of the suffering that is to come is also difficult for us to see. We try to take very good care of Her. She lives. She breathes.

She is like all *Wakan Tanka's* creations. She is fully alive and the very expression of *Wakan Tanka's* love.

"He gave us *Ina Maka* and She is our home. She is sacred and a special place for all creation to learn and mature their souls. We pray and beseech the Creator to spare Her illness and suffering. Keep praying for her, *Zintkala Zi Win.*"

The *Wakiyan* spoke these words while experiencing great distress themselves. They went back into the clouds. It was the end of this part of the vision. I listened intently as their thundering claps rolled away into the night.

15

PTESAN WIN

You are wrapped

In compassion

You honor me

By your presence

My heart jumps

In heavenly joy

And I am humbled

Beyond all

Earthly emotion

Oh, White Buffalo Calf Woman

To you I give

A promise most heartfelt

To you

I will forever listen

To you

I will forever follow.

The darkness of night still enveloped me. I sat a while on my buffalo hide and prayed with my *Canunpa Wakan* for *Ina Maka*. Sadness filled my heart and I hoped none of the bad would ever find Her. The stars slowly faded from view and I realized more clouds were rolling in.

I heard the *Wakiyan* thunder across the skies with loud crashes and giant bangs of sound. They lit up the night sky with great intensity and made their presence known in powerful streaks of *Wakan Tanka's* energy and light. I listened carefully, knowing it was time for another vision as the loud crashes turned into thundering hooves. I realized herds of *tatanka* were running in great numbers across the land and through the night.

The *Wakiyan* approached quickly, flashing white light across the herds and illuminating the animals with flashes. I heard them speak to me through the sounds of hooves pounding the land.

"As the coming time approaches," the *Wakiyan* began, "you will hear the intense thundering of hooves as the *tatanka* run with great energy. You will see masses of *tatanka* herds come together and run in immense bands across the lands. Out of the herds will come the *Tatanka Ska* (White Buffalo) and *Ptesan Win* (White Buffalo Calf Woman).

"When you see and hear the *tatanka* running in great massive herds, it will startle you. That's when you will know that *Ptesan Win* wants to give you very important instructions. She will appear from the *tatanka* herds and you will immediately need to listen to Her from your soul. Pay careful attention. Heed Her directions and do all that She asks you to do, and in the time and order that She asks. She will lead you from danger. She will guide you and help you know the timing of things and when and where to go with your people.

"She will appear to others as well, and they will be lead to places of safety. You will know some of the people that She appears to, and some will be your friends. Be very careful. Do not let anyone else influence what you see and hear or give you conflicting information about the instructions that She has brought to you. At times, it will be easy to be influenced by others because there will be great confusion and fear. Do not let this happen. Remember, *Zintkala Zi Win*, who you are, a helper for your people. This will not be a time of comparison of information. Truly believe in yourself. Believe. Believe. Believe."

As the *Wakiyan* finished speaking, I looked towards the North where I continued to hear pounding hooves. And then I saw Her. She suddenly appeared before me. Her hair was long and black, almost to Her knees. She was dressed in pure white buffalo skins. I instantly knew She was *Ptesan Win*. She was very beautiful with a radiant white light around Her. She approached me in a loving, gentle way. I sat quietly transfixed by Her. An energy of pure love and compassion enveloped Her, and I felt my heart pound as it responded to Her. My body surrendered, and I felt profoundly peaceful.

"*Zintkala Zi Win*," she began in a soft voice. "You will lead your people. You will see what to do through vision. Whenever you hear the pounding hooves of the *tatanka*, stop and listen. It could come anytime, day or night. You will know by the sound to stop and immediately pay attention. Then you will see me.

"I will give you instructions. Sometimes what I tell you will come to you very fast and I will ask you to act quickly. Remember, on the earthly plane, many things appear to manifest at the last moment. In reality, what is to manifest has taken a long time and has been waiting to appear from the spirit side. That is why it looks like it was fast when it really wasn't. Remember this so you don't question things in your mind when asked to take actions very swiftly. It means that the correct time for the manifestation to appear on Earth from the spirit side is either happening or fast approaching.

"Always pray with your *Canunpa Wakan* and do not question anything seen from vision. You will know, and you will know very strongly."

I thanked *Ptesan Win* over and over for giving me this special vision. I told Her I would listen very carefully when I heard the *tatanka* run. I expressed my deep gratitude to be able to see and hear Her. I felt so honored to be in Her presence. I promised Her I would do all that She asked and as quickly as She asked.

"You are allowed to see the future of the coming time, *Zintkala Zi Win,* to help your people. This is a special honor given to very few. One day you will understand why you were chosen to receive visions of such an insightful nature. One day you will be told. One day you will know."

I opened my mouth to say *"wopila"* out loud, but realized She was suddenly gone. A white mist had encircled Her, unnoticed by me until that moment. I heard the *tatanka* herds as they charged their hooves into the land and the *Wakiyan* fired across the blackened skies in an untamed chorus of awe and might.

"*Wopila, wopila, wopila, wopila,*" I cried out into the blackness.

16

FLYING HIGH

In the sky
I looked down
And saw beauty
Unseen before
Lush greenery
Plants as tall as
Trees used to be
Giant flowers open
To the sun
In brilliant array
Human dwellings
Luminous and shining
Love and peace
Floated up to me
Compassion hung
In the air
I was overcome
With wonderment

And then I remembered
Wakan Tanka's prophecy
The promise shown me
The foretelling
Of the New Earth
Yet to be realized.

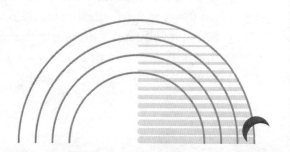

It grew colder. I pulled the thick buffalo hide around my shoulders and prayed for warmth. The *Wakiyan* came back and flashed their lightning all around me. In an instant, the *Wakiyan* lifted me high in the sky for the next part of my vision.

I was happy flying with them. I felt free, open, and unrestricted. We flew through a gentle mist and then I saw breathtaking beauty below me. For a moment, I wondered if we were on another planet. They told me to keep looking down because what I was being shown was the New Earth yet to come.

"*Wakan Tanka* will bring a new time to the Earth," they began. "All humans that remain on *Ina Maka* will have souls cleansed like babies. They will start again no matter their physical age. They will look like the previous age they were on Earth, but their souls will suddenly be in a new time, so they can start again.

"The planet will exist to emanate love, peace, and learning. This will be the rebirth told by prophecy and the awakening described by the Benevolent Spirits of the past. It will be the time when souls who remain from the old look forward to the great change into the new.

"When conditions look bleak, *Zintkala Zi Win*, remember that love and peace are soon to reign, and hold this in your heart. Remember the promise of the New Earth and hold those images in your mind. It will give you hope.

"As the coming time approaches, there will be many difficult trials. Those that know and understand *Wakan Tanka's* plan will get through it in amazing ways. Those that fight it and cannot accept it will cause suffering to themselves and others. Countless things of the world will be dissolved. Many people will turn away from *Wakan Tanka*, their Creator, rather than running to Him.

They will be so fearful and confused that they will wonder if the Creator is gone. It will be *Wakan Tanka* who decides the way of the future and not humankind.

"*Wakan Tanka* will lead Earth and all Her inhabitants to a state of being that is much better—one of love and kindness, one of peace and compassion and one of individual learning and growth.

"Vast and far-reaching change will be very difficult for some people. They will cling to the past and want their lives to be like they were. It was a world they understood and one that generations built. *Wakan Tanka's* will and vision will prevail to create a world no human on Earth will be able to visualize. It will be a New Earth that no humans have ever before seen or experienced. It will be a beautiful world far better and without evil.

"To those who do believe and keep their faith in *Wakan Tanka,* their hearts will be filled with hope that a New Earth and a new time will be a much better place. To those that despair, their suffering will settle in their hearts, and with it, terrible fear. The Creator does not want any human to suffer in this way."

The *Wakiyan* let me see the new *Ina Maka* just below us as we flew fast across the skies. Everything looked so peaceful and loving, including humans and animals. The plants were taller and more lush. It was like all creation was smiling. I felt deep love and unending peace rise up to meet us. We flew a little further and I saw human dwellings that were luminous and beautiful unlike anything I had ever seen.

I felt happy and positive looking downward at the New Earth. My heart was filled with love, and I wished *Ina Maka* could be like this immediately.

"*Zintkala Zi Win,*" the *Wakiyan* called me directly. "You must do away with any fear or worry about the future yourself. Remember this. It is natural for earthly human beings to have some fear, but now you have seen what is going to happen and how beautiful it will be. You will be a leader of your people. You will need to be very strong. Very loving. Very patient. Yours is a lifelong duty of giving hope and promise to your people. You will need to maintain great courage and faith as you have been trained to do.

"Learn to pay no attention to those who make negative accusations about you or build you up positively to be more than you are. Remain neutral and humble. Only *Wakan Tanka* knows what is truly in a person's heart and soul.

"Pray and believe that people will be touched by your words and at times even healed by them. Words are very powerful and creative. They manifest entire realities. They are little seeds of inspiration and vision.

"Choose your words and your thoughts carefully. If you let words or thoughts become negative they can overcome you and manifest something you did not want created. Be very mindful of every word.

"We have shown you portions of the New Earth. You will see added visions. But first we need to show you more of the transition to the coming time. As *Wakan Tanka* pushes the New Earth into manifestation, there will be great turbulence and destruction. *Ina Maka* will be much sicker than She was supposed to be as the transition time arrives. This will cause far more suffering for Her and all who inhabit Her than would have been necessary if She had been allowed to stay healthy.

"Remember this, *Zintkala Zi Win,* and keep your heart and soul on the new era, the new beginning, the New Earth that is to come."

"*Waste*," I replied. "I will do as you ask. *Wopila. Wopila.*"

17

WHEN POWERS
Of the Universe
Cause earthly panic
Humans will listen
With the ears
Of their hearts
And the walk
Of their souls.

I was still high in the skies with the *Wakiyan*. Dark storm clouds appeared before us, yet we did not slow down or fly around them. The storm was violent, and I was scared as we flew right through the tormented winds. I felt a shift in energy and realized I was feeling an unusual sense of panic coming up to meet us from the land below.

We arrived at the other end of the storm and I saw vast lands and waters beneath me. We flew so fast and so far that I had no idea where we were, nor could I recognize anything. People appeared below that I did not recognize by their clothing or their faces or how they lived. I remembered a time that *Unci* had told me that many different kinds and colors of people, animals, and plants lived on *Ina Maka*.

The *Wakiyan* interrupted my thoughts with a warning: "We need to show you the immensity of the destruction that will take place when *Wakan Tanka* gives His order," they began. "First you will hear and feel the vibrations of the *tatanka* herds running. Then you will see them. Buffalo herds will be seen running for miles and miles. Many herds will unite and run together. All living on planet Earth will recognize this as being very unusual.

"The buffalo will be the first to be seen. They will be followed by all the four-legged *wamakaskan* (animals) as they too will join together in enormous herds and run. People will know instinctively that the *wamakaskan* stampedes are extremely unusual and it will cause panic. As the stampedes continue, it will feel like a universal rebellion to people and cause more and more panic.

"The spirit of *Wakan Tanka* will suddenly appear in all the *wamakaskan* and they will continue stampeding. A massive vibration will pulsate around the world. It will cause armies of humans to be driven to run, to charge, to once and for all defeat their enemies.

"Great armies of every nation will pick up their weapons and charge. There will be no specific orders given and there will be no stopping them. Massive armies of soldiers will run at each other and heave their weapons upon their enemies. As they do, the Earth will open, and all the armies will fall into huge pits which will dissolve them immediately. They will take their weapons with them and those too will be dissolved into *Ina Maka*. It won't matter how advanced the weaponry or how hard the armies fight. They will be gone forever.

"The winged *zintkala* (birds) will suddenly take flight at the same time and form aerial formations in the skies all over the world. The flying will be started by the *wanbli oyate* (eagle people). They will vibrate millions of feathered wings that will fly together across the Earth and cause man-made birds to take flight in support. The armies of the air will be met by huge *tate'* (winds). These winds will appear suddenly and be so fierce that the man-made birds will be blown apart and scatter their remains into huge, smoldering pits. *Ina Maka* will take them into the pits and destroy them.

"The *hogan* (fish), the whales, and the dolphins will start the stampede of the waters and seas by joining forces and swimming together in massive formations. The energy they create will cause fleets of ships to race across the waters to support their armies of war. Great enormous waves will be sent to the ships, which will destroy them, and their remains will be scattered. As they sink into the waters, great pits will open below the seas and *Ina Maka* will swallow them. The ships will sink to the Great Mother's core where She will burn everything, and they will be no more.

"In the coming time, *Wakan Tanka* will not allow terrible weapons to exist in the world. He will show humankind that their minds cannot contain the evil of war and mass destruction. *Wakan Tanka* will destroy all weapons. The great vibration weapon that is to come disturbs Him the most. Using vibrations, it interferes with all living species, including their very essence. Evil will use the vibration weapon to destroy God's creations, including humans, His animals, His plant life, and finally, the entire planet. *Wakan Tanka* will not allow this to happen.

"*Wakan Tanka* is very disappointed that humankind has traveled so far down the path of destruction and hatred rather than the path of love. He will rid humans of the great vibration weapon, all weapons, all wars, and will remove them from humans' memories.

"The time of destruction will be very frightening for the world. There will be much turmoil and terror. *Wakan Tanka* will lead good hearts to special places on the Earth where they will be safe. He will protect them with things unseen. Legions of *Wakan Tanka's* Benevolent Spirits will put up spiritual shields protecting goodhearted people.

"Some people will see *Wakan Tanka's* spirits, but most will not. Some will feel their presence and continue to turn to the Creator. All will be surprised how beautifully *Wakan Tanka* takes care of His people. All will be amazed.

"During this time, *Zintkala Zi Win,* you will be instructed. You will be told how to lead the people and how to comfort them. They will have places to live, food to eat, and water to drink. You will be told where to go. Watch for the signs. Watch the *tatanka* herds. They will know. They will start the charge. We *Wakiyan* will pound the Earth when *Wakan Tanka* tells us to begin and we will command the *Tatanka Oyate* (Buffalo People) to start their stampedes. Watch the *tatanka.* They will be your first sign."

The *Wakiyan* had previously shown me enormous evil, including people and demons in fiery pits. I realized the destruction to get rid of evil would be very extensive and I suddenly felt tired and numb. I knew *Wakan Tanka's* annihilation of evil needed to be done and I believed His ways were always right. I felt sick to my stomach and was unable to feel anything but intense sadness.

The *Wakiyan* and I flew back to the *Hanbleceya* place, and I was gently placed on the buffalo hide. Seeing my sadness, they lovingly advised me.

"Think only of the new way of life that *Wakan Tanka* is bringing. Life on *Ina Maka* will be full of peace and love. Think only of the beauty that is coming."

I watched the *Wakiyan* fly into the night's blackness as the vision they brought ended. They rode with bursts of lightning and crashes of thunder. I wrapped the buffalo robe around me and prayed in complete thankfulness for *Wakan Tanka's* powerful ways.

I looked around and surrendered to the shadows of the night. Everything was very quiet and serene. Little stars twinkled from above, and gentle breezes twirled around me.

I was at peace in the engulfing tranquility. The darkness was like a soft blanket that wrapped me in protection. I thought about my first day and night of *Hanbleceya* and felt very blessed and grateful.

18

GRANDMOTHER

I love you
I honor you
I thank you
Without you
I would be
Lost and afraid
An orphan
On her own
Wakan Tanka
I pray for *Unci*
May her great love
Be given
Back to her
Again and again
Wopila Unci
Wopila Unci.

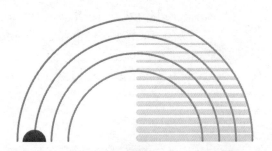

It was the second day of my *Hanbleceya*. Dawn's lovely fingers of orange light spread across the land. I welcomed the first light of the sun while thinking about the visions I'd been shown during the night.

"*Hihanni waste'* (good morning)," *Unci* called to me.

I hadn't seen her coming up the hillside and was happy to hear her voice.

"*Hihanni waste',*" I called back.

Unci walked up to where I was sitting slightly out of breath. "*Tonituka he* (how are you)?"

"*Matanyan* (I am fine)," I replied.

"I came to see how you are. I heard spirit *tatanka* running. It must be part of your vision."

"*Han, han* (yes, yes)," I replied. "*Unci*, I saw *Ptesan Win*! She came out of the *tatanka* herd and talked to me!"

"You are very honored. This is a most powerful and beautiful vision. Keep everything you see and hear tucked away in your heart and soul. Never let it go. Hold onto it forever. Visions are the most precious of all gifts a human being can receive from the Creator. Your vision is more valuable than anything on this earthly plane. Some people have honored their visions so deeply in their souls that their visions have followed them from lifetime to lifetime. It is the will of *Wakan Tanka* if it is to be so. I have a feeling that you may be one of those special people."

I felt honored to hear *Unci's* words, but also a little anxious. I wondered if I were really worthy to see such important visions.

"*Unci*, I am a young person and I feel like it's a big vision. Some of the vision is hard to see and some of it is very beautiful. Are you sure this was meant for me?"

Unci gave me a big reassuring smile, then replied, "Only *Wakan Tanka* knows who carries visions of importance for the people and who does not. All people have special gifts and talents from the Creator. Being a seer of sacred visions is yours. I was told you were to be a medicine woman and a holy woman. I've raised you and taught you in these sacred ways because of the visions I was given by *Wakan Tanka* about you. I am not surprised that He has chosen you to have an important vision for our people."

I nodded as her words rolled over me.

"*Zintkala Zi Win*," she said as she looked me firmly in the eyes, "doubt is an enemy of vision. You are a young adult and so you question. It's okay at your age. But now I must insist that doubts can have no room in your mind and spirit as you go forward during your *Hanbleceya*. You are in ceremony. There can be no questions when you are given visions from *Wakan Tanka* and his helpers at this time."

"Oh *Unci*," I replied. "You have taught me the lesson of doubt many times and I know I cannot let my mind go there. These doubts came over me so fast that I didn't even realize they were there before I started expressing them."

I hung my head, realizing my mistake, and felt remorseful for even saying them out loud. *Unci* reached out her hand to me and lifted my chin. She smiled and nodded her great love and approval of me.

"We are human and not perfect," she slowly began. "It is better to express what you feel to me as your teacher. Do you see how easy it is for the earthly mind to go where it doesn't need to go? Since we know we are imperfect we must practice every day to keep our minds focused on where they need to be. And that focus needs to be on *Wakan Tanka* and gratitude for allowing us to walk in His grace."

"*Han, Unci*," I humbly replied.

"You are forgiven by the Creator and always by me," she said, flashing a big smile. "Thank you for sharing your feelings with me. Now you can go forward again receiving your visions and knowing to keep your earthly mind in check. These visions are all about your soul. Remember that."

"*Han, Unci*," I said as I smiled back at her. I felt like a rock had suddenly been lifted from me.

"*Waste'*," *Unci* said comfortingly. "When we bring you down from the hill at the end of four days, we will have an *Inipi*. After that, you may talk to me about your visions so I can help you interpret what you've seen, and help you learn how to carry this vision in your life. As you know, you will only talk to me, your teacher, about your vision. If it's to be different, *Wakan Tanka* will instruct you through prayer."

"*Han, Unci. Wopila*," I replied.

A sweet peace swept over me. I felt very humbled by all that I had seen and heard. I had been reminded to put my total faith and belief in *Wakan Tanka* and not to question the vision. I remembered *Unci*'s teachings—that to question *Wakan Tanka* with doubt and disbelief was very insulting to Him. I prayed to keep my mind free of questions and not to doubt any of the visions. I asked *Wakan Tanka* to help my earthly mind stay out of the way.

Unci had taught me to say *wopila* (thank you) over and over in my mind when questions arose about the precious gift of *Wakan Tanka*'s visions. She taught me to repeat *wopila* so that I focused on gratitude until the questioning went away. She also taught me to repeat *wopila* in my mind when the spirits gave instructions for healings and not to question their instructions.

I learned gratitude as a little child by saying *wopila* at each new dawn while sitting quietly with my Grandmother as the first twinkling of each day gently peeked over the horizon. We said *wopila* to *Wakan Tanka* every morning and every evening.

I said *wopila* many times in my mind during each day. As I became older, I grew in humility and deep gratitude and I thanked the Creator for everything in my life. Thanking Him over and over did not seem enough to do for all that He had given me.

Unci's words floated over me and I focused my mind back on her rather than on remembering some of the many teachings she had given me from the time I was a very young child.

"Keep remembering all the details of each part of your vision. Bravely face whatever is shown you. We are praying for you at the bottom of the hill and we're keeping the fire going for you also."

"Wopila, wopila, wopila, wopila," I whispered to Unci.

She gave me another big smile and began singing a sacred song as she turned away and walked down the side of the mountain.

I smiled back at her as she left. I loved her so deeply. During my ceremony of Hanbleceya, I felt even more love and reverence for her. I realized how much she had influenced my life, how carefully she had taught me, and how much she had given me. I owed everything to her and to Wakan Tanka.

"Wopila Wakan Tanka for blessing me with such a beautiful loving human being."

I lifted my Canunpa Wakan to the skies and thanked Him for the precious gift of my Unci.

19

ANGELIC CHOIRS

Wonderful harmonies

Unknown on Earth

Hearken through the skies

Beautiful love and peace

Beyond grasp

Arise all around

Stunning luminous

Lights of every color

Appear and inspire rapture

And then

The Angel appears.

"L egions of *Ogligle Wakan* (Sacred Angel) will be sent by *Wakan Tanka* to Earth!" a voice declared loudly.

I was praying when I heard the words. I was startled and peeked out with one eye. Immediately I heard magnificent voices singing from above as if they were coming from the clouds. The area all around me was bathed in dazzling white light. I felt love and harmony fall over me like a beautiful blanket and was suspended in serene awe. I realized the vision was showing itself again.

A luminous figure appeared and slowly walked toward me. He stopped in front of me. I had never seen such brilliance. He was dressed in white buckskins and was much taller than a human man. Glowing white light bounced off him, making it difficult for me to see him clearly. Perfect love and compassion surrounded him, and I immediately fell into divine peace.

"I am an *Ogligle Wakan* sent by *Wakan Tanka*," he began in a deep and unearthly sounding voice.

I remembered *Unci* instructing me about the *Ogligle Wakan*.

He softened his voice as he continued. "*Zintkala Zi Win*, I have come to show you a part of the coming time when we *Ogligle Wakan* will be called to help *Wakan Tanka* rid the planet Earth of evil. You must understand that our numbers are mighty, and we are formed by divisions of service to *Wakan Tanka*. I need to show you the mighty battles which are not pleasant to see. That's because we warrior *Ogligle Wakan* will be sent to Earth for the great battle against evil that is to come.

"The sacred *Ogligle Wakan* are spiritual warriors of supreme importance who will take evil out of humankind and all earthly life. This includes demons and other forms of evil that cannot be seen by the human eye. They will take any infection of evil out of *Ina Maka* as well. They will take the evil while screaming in protest to the upper skies and into space where they will dissolve it with great fireballs. When they are done, there will be nothing left of the evil which now plagues the Earth.

"Some on Earth will be able to see the Great Battles. Most people will not, but will still feel the results. The *Wakiyan* will assist the *Ogligle Wakan*. To most people on Earth, it will appear like there are many fierce storms which will be loud and very disturbing. At times, horrible screeches and screams will be heard as the evil is taken away. The sounds of demons will be mixed with thunder, but louder that the most immense thunderbolts.

"People will be very frightened as they realize there is a battle in the skies. Remarkable lights will appear in the Heavens. Flashes will materialize as evil is destroyed by giant fireballs. Massive strikes of lightning will be heard and seen. Explosions in the air will be felt, seen, and heard. The demons and all evil will be disintegrated into pieces never again to reside on Earth.

"Legions of *Ogligle Wakan* will protect all peoples as they gather at safe places on Earth. These protected people will be spared so that life can go on.

"All memories of evil, of pain, of fear and loss will be removed from peoples' minds. It will be as if they were born again. They will know who and what they were on planet Earth, but they will remember only the good.

"The Benevolent Spirits from other dimensions will arrive to help. Some, *Zintkala Zi Win,* you have already seen. You will know and recognize them. They will help you. They will tell you how to help your people, so they know what to do and how to protect themselves. They will give hope to the people for the wonderful future that is to come."

The vision the *Ogligle Wakan* gave me was overwhelming. I realized I was staring right at him while trying to take in everything he said. I quickly dropped my eyes as a sign of respect as I had been taught.

"*Wopila, wopila, wopila, wopila,*" I softly answered him. "I am very honored and will keep all that you have told me deep in my soul."

He paused for a moment, and I realized he sent me a wave of warmth and love. I was immediately engulfed in his beautiful light and felt his magnificent blessing.

20

EVIL SPIRITS

Unseen by humans

Their infection

In all places

On Earth

Pulverized

In mid air

By legions

Of warrior angels

Evil never seen

Never heard

Never ever again.

The *Ogligle Wakan* let me rest for a few minutes, then he allowed the vision to continue.

"The chief of the *Ogligle Wakan* shall order his legions to sound their flutes and pound their drums in a chorus of great discord. The evil ones will hear the overwhelming sounds and be very afraid!"

The *Ogligle Wakan* made his announcement again using his deep and unearthly sounding voice. I realized my attention had drifted to the beautiful love he had sent me, and I put my mind back on what he was saying.

He continued in a softer voice. "Only evil will be able to actually hear the flutes and drums from the *Ogligle Wakan*. The sounds will cause waves of vibrations and all forms of evil, including demons and negative spirits, will be driven insane by the unearthly loud noises.

"Without being able to think about actions to retaliate, the evil ones will be forced to leave the bodies of those they torment and follow the sounds. Suddenly millions of *Ogligle Wakan* and advanced spirits, eagle spirits, animal spirits, and spirit helpers will force the evil to outer space. A blasting from torrential sound vibrations will dissolve all evil into nothingness.

"The warrior *Ogligle Wakan* and the *Wanbli Gleska* fight evil in space using sounds and vibrations to pulverize it. The *Wakiyan* fight their battles with the storms of the planet and force evil into giant pits and *Ina Maka* dissolves it in Her inner core. All peoples will help get rid of evil in the coming time in the way they are instructed.

"Humans who have been possessed by evil will collapse. These victims of evil will be taken to special places and doctored. The

Ogligle Wakan and spirit helpers will know who has been a victim of evil and who has continuously called evil to them. Many people will be restored to their original state before being taken over by evil and will experience love and peace.

"Some humans will be so devastated by the loss of their evil spirits and the power they seemingly brought that they will keep calling them to come back. These humans will not be rehabilitated and will be quickly separated from others. *Wakan Tanka* wants all His children to return to their original state of love. Those who repeatedly call evil to them will be sent to another place.

"A large pit will open beneath humans on Earth wanting evil to walk with them. The Earth Mother will very quickly swallow them. They will be taken to Her inner core, where they will be no more. *Ina Maka* will burn them and be cleansed of them forever."

The *Ogligle Wakan* paused. I immediately tried to imagine the Earth and all Her inhabitants free of evil. Grandmother had taught me that evil and good were always present on the planet and we needed to carefully navigate our lives so that we would not be swept up by evil. We tried to stay in *waste'* (good) in all our human endeavors.

The *Ogligle Wakan* continued. "There is a coming time when *Wakan Tanka* will usher in a new era on the Earth. This was always in His plan. He gave humankind free will to create more of the good for the coming time. He wanted humans to expand upon His own original creation.

"Many humans have created good on the planet and will continue to do so. But more humans will allow evil to take them over. By the time the new era is to be manifested, humans will have gone backwards in their growth toward the good. As a result, they will be in danger of destroying themselves and the Earth Mother. *Wakan Tanka* has seen that humankind will destroy themselves and all His creation if they continue their current path. In the coming time, it will be more painful for the planet Earth and Her inhabitants to go through the transition of the new era than it would have been if Earth had never been heavily taken over by evil.

"*Wakan Tanka's* new era will be a time for peace and love to rule. He will restore the Earth to Her original nature. She will need to be cleansed from the inhabitation of evil and will also need great healing and restoration.

"Because of the behavior of humans, evil will have heavily inhabited *Ina Maka*. She will be infected by evil through the pollution of the Earth, the destruction of the skies, and the destruction of Her beauty. Humans will have taken from Her for so long without giving anything back that She will be decimated in many areas. They will have taken from Her year after year without considering the consequences, as your people have done for seven generations.

"*Ina Maka* has been home to man, animals, birds, plants, water, rocks, and winds. It will take considerable time to restore Her back to health. Once the new era has happened and She has been healed, She will provide complete love, peace, and protection for all Her children."

The *Ogligle Wakan* paused and sent me a warm, reassuring breeze.

"*Wopila, wopila, wopila, wopila,*" I heartily called out to him.

He continued his warm, loving blessing and another wave of lovely peace swept over me.

21

WAKAN TANKA

Almighty God
Of great love
Understanding
And compassion
Of healing
And forgiveness
Of resurrection
And restoration
Wakan Tanka
I pray to see You
In the beautiful time

The *Ogligle Wakan* paused very briefly, then continued showing me the vision.

"The *Wakiyan* and the *Wanbli Gleska* will play a major role in restoring *Ina Maka*!"

As he spoke, I saw large flocks of *Wanbli Gleska* fly rapidly across the skies as the *Wakiyan* followed in unwavering pursuit of evil. The very sight of millions of eagles and the flashes of lightning all around was fierce and breathtakingly beautiful all at the same time.

"The Creator will send millions of *Wakiyan* to assist the *Ogligle Wakan*. They will run across the Earth like herds of stampeding wild horses. They will strike powerfully many more times than ever before seen. They will energize *Ina Maka* and help Her to restore Herself. They will concentrate in areas of need and where there has been much damage to the Mother.

"The *Wakiyan* will be full of creative energy and healing. They will provide the energized strikes for creation and visions. When they flash across the Earth, it will be thrilling and frightening at the same time.

"*Zintkala Zi Win*, your medicine will be of the *Wakiyan*. They want to help you so you can assist your people with healings. Lightning is the medicine of visions. It is the medicine of creation and of creating new beginnings. It is the song of bringing something new into existence. When you want a healing for someone, an answer to know how to lead, or blessings to move forward, always ask the *Wakiyan* and they will help you."

"*Wopila, wopila, wopila, wopila*," I said gratefully to the *Ogligle Wakan*.

"The *Wanbli Gleska* are very important to your *Lakota* people," began the *Ogligle Wakan*. "They too will play a very important part in the healing of *Ina Maka*. Watch the *Wanbli Gleska,* as they will also be responsible for starting the healing process. You will hear and feel a huge flapping of wings as they create powerful vibrations. The *zintkala* (birds) of the air will flap their mighty wings in unison with the *wanbli* (eagles). They will fly and sing as one as they open a symphony in the skies. They will create astounding vibrations that spread across the planet.

"The *Wanbli Gleska* will announce their coming with songs of symphony to you. *Zintkala Zi Win,* listen for them to come. All of humankind will fall on their knees in reverence for this beautiful event. The *Wanbli Gleska* of the air will be the first to herald in a new beginning. They will escort the Benevolent Ones onto Earth from the upper Heavens to help humankind begin again.

"The Benevolent Ones will descend directly to the special places on Earth that were provided for people before the upheavals took place. They will help humans start the renewal process.

"Humans will be very grateful. Together, they will begin the building of a new civilization based on love and peace. The Benevolent Ones will lead all of humankind. This will be a wonderful time of renewal, and people will rejoice with love, joy and laughter.

"The vibration of all the *zintkala* singing together will cause humans' memories of evil and bad to be erased. They will remember only love, peace and compassion. As the Benevolent Ones descend, people will be transformed mentally and spiritually and be ready to build a civilization based on love for all of life."

My human mind began to wonder when all of this was going to happen. I hadn't even had the thought before. The *Ogligle Wakan* was showing me that I had a part to play and I felt honored even being considered for such responsibility. I wondered how old I would be when the new era began.

As if reading my mind, the *Ogligle Wakan* asked me if I wanted to know when all he had told me was going to happen. I nodded yes.

He responded carefully. "This question of when is something I want to get out of your mind. I don't know when. No one does. Only *Wakan Tanka* knows. I don't know if it will be in your lifetime now or in other lifetimes in the future. The one thing I do know is that *Wakan Tanka* is preparing you for the time that is to come. He wants you to hold these visions deeply in your soul.

"It is better this way. You've been given the signs to look for and you'll be told where to lead your people. You've been chosen because of your faith and belief in *Wakan Tanka's* ways. When you truly believe, it is much easier to receive the heavenly messages that are sent. We know you genuinely understand this.

"There will be hard times, but the coming time of peace and love will be more beautiful than anything ever seen on Earth before. It is best to hold the visions of the peaceful and loving Earth in your heart and never ask the questions of when or why to *Wakan Tanka*."

I nodded and tried to hold all that he had shown me in my soul as he paused again.

22

MITAKUYE OYASIN

We are all related

To all life

We are one

Together in love

Of all people

All plants

All animals

Mother Earth

Father Sky

The four winds

All are related

To us as one

Bound to each other

By the Creator

In love, respect

And compassion

Forever together

I pray all humans

Will come to believe

This divine truth.

The *Ogligle Wakan* lowered his head for a moment. His luminescent light was so prevalent that it flooded me in beautiful white as well.

He looked up and started his next instruction of the vision. "*Ptesan Win* is the daughter of *Wakan Tanka*. In the coming time, She will come back to Earth after the destruction of all evil. She will lead many of the Benevolent Ones as they all come to help bring new life to Earth. The Benevolent Ones are very advanced souls who are now spirits working for *Wakan Tanka*. Some once lived on Earth and others lived on other planets.

"*Ptesan Win* will descend in a physical body from the Heavens. She will be escorted by thousands of *Wanbli Gleska* to the earthly plane. The Benevolent Ones will follow Her, also in physical bodies. They will be seen among beautiful celestial lights and choirs of holy songs as they descend from the skies.

"*Ptesan Win* will be seen in many places on the planet at the same time. She will hold all captive by Her heavenly beauty, Her boundless love, and Her emanating peace. She will usher in new ways to live on Earth based on *Wakan Tanka's* manifestation of healing and restoration for *Ina Maka* and all Her inhabitants.

"All humans will weep at Her coming. They will feel embraced by Her kindness and the beautiful hope that She and the Benevolent Ones create. She will oversee immense centers of learning. The Benevolent Ones will teach the people how to love more, find more peace within themselves, and how to create wonderful new lives.

"People will be taught how to conduct their behavior so that it benefits all humanity and creates new realities of love, healing, and peace. They will realize there is enough for all life. Earth will not need to be plundered and destroyed for humankind to get ahead. They will learn to create ways that do no harm to *Ina Maka,* Her animals, plants, and other humans.

"People will turn to *Wakan Tanka* and the divisions of religion, race, and culture will fall away. Old hatreds will be erased in all humans' minds. They will learn to embrace the *Lakota* philosophy of living, which is '*Mitakuye Oyasin*' (All My Relations), which means all people are related and are one together, including animals, birds, Mother Earth and all life.

"In the new era of peace and love, life will be very different. *Ina Maka* will be restored to Her beauty and bounty. All humans will walk in harmony with the Mother.

"The Benevolent Ones will show humankind how to build dwellings that look like large crystals. Many will be round, some will be square with rounded edges, and others will be very tall. The dwellings will be porous, so they can let in fresh air. They will also be nonporous at times to keep cold or hot air out. The buildings will be translucent. There will be no visible braces or beams. They will be heated by the sun and cooled by avoiding the sun. They will use earthly elements to maintain them that can be reused over and over. They will be extraordinarily beautiful and radiant.

"The dwellings and other needs of humans will be made of materials that do no harm to *Ina Maka* or Her inhabitants. The use of new materials will be taught by the Benevolent Ones and are unknown in your day. Everything that humans create will do no harm to *Ina Maka* or any of *Wakan Tanka's* creatures. Peoples' minds will be turned only to love and peace, and their creations will reflect this different way of thinking. Humankind will be able to create far beyond anything imagined in previous times.

"*Ptesan Win* and the Benevolent Ones will help show humankind many new ways of living. They will work with humans for a long time and establish enduring love and peace. When they have finished, they will depart from the Earth. The

Wanbli Gleska will escort *Ptesan Win* and the Benevolent Ones from the earthly realm as they go back into the Heavens."

The *Ogligle Wakan* paused as if picturing the glorious ascent of *Ptesan Win* and the Benevolent Ones back into the heavenly sphere. I could see that he had much love and respect for Her.

The *Ogligle Wakan* looked back at me and continued the vision. "Life on Earth will be very different, and humans will also have a complete change from the way they were before. They will continue to expand upon all they have learned and will keep improving their lives. They will learn to never inflict harm on the Earth Mother or any living thing.

"Humankind will still be born, live, and die. Humans will be on Earth to glorify their souls and learn how to love and lead better lives. There will still be sicknesses, but most will be degenerative conditions due to aging or organisms. They will not be due to demon possession or the spread of serious infectious diseases planted by evil.

"At first, as *Ina Maka* is healing, the extremes on the planet will be part of life. Once She is in a more healed state, the planet will gradually become more temperate everywhere. There won't be as many extremes such as heat and cold, dry and flooded, excessive storms or no storms.

"There will be a balance in the growing of crops and more cooperation from *Ina Maka* and the *Wakiyan* by giving adequate rains when needed.

"In a world of love and peace, there will be no carnivores. They will exist on Earth, but the Mother will provide new food for sustenance, so they don't have to kill.

"The balance of animal life and human life will be maintained in natural ways and by the numbers born into the world. When all is in balance, species don't have to reproduce massively for survival.

"There will be no killing, including colossal, disastrous wars. When people have disagreements, they will settle them within a justice system which is local and worldly at the same time.

The justice system will be run by the Benevolent Ones in the beginning, and then by humans who have been taught the new system of peace and love. Disagreements will be resolved out of love and respect by both sides who will want the best for all humankind as their goal.

"There will be many colors and kinds of humans, all sizes, all shapes, all cultures. Love will prevail. The system of love and peace will unite all peoples as one and they will enjoy their differences.

"There will be dwellings for the sick which will be loving places of healing. Patients will participate in the ceremonies of *Ptesan Win,* including sweat lodges and sun dances. The sick will be restored back to health with careful nurturing."

The *Ogligle Wakan* paused and looked directly into my eyes. "It will be wonderful to live with our Earth Mother in this coming time don't you think, *Zintkala Zi Win?*"

"*Han, han* (yes, yes). I hope the time is soon," I replied happily, still seeing the vision he had shown me.

"Always remember, *Zintkala Zi Win,* time and the question of when is never clear from the heavenly plane to us. It gets distorted. It is *Wakan Tanka's* way and only He knows the timing that is to come."

He smiled lovingly at me as I nodded in understanding.

23

ANGEL SPIRITS

Warriors of *waste'*
Warriors of the good
The power from God
To help win
The battle over evil
Angel Spirits
With power of the good
Help us all
To walk in your way
The way of *waste'*.

He took several deep breaths, then continued the vision. "Before I leave you, I want to help you better understand the evil that will be on Earth in the coming time." the *Ogligle Wakan* spoke in a soft manner. "I know you don't have much knowledge of evil at your young age, though you're already learning from your Grandmother and your medicine work how to fight demons."

As he finished speaking, I saw streaks of brilliant light like numerous comets coming down quickly to join us. Several more *Ogligle Wakan* appeared out of the lights. They sang in a rapturous chorus as they surrounded us in a protected circle. Immediately I felt immense joy and experienced their radiant blessings. They stood beaming at us as the *Ogligle Wakan* continued instructing me.

"*Zintkala Zi Win,* there are many planets in *Wakan Tanka's* infinite universe. Some of these planets have established civilizations based entirely on love, peace and compassion. They walk in the way of *waste'*. They are very far ahead of planet Earth. *Wakan Tanka* wants Earth to be like them.

"Earth is a planet that has a long way to go before it can be like the others. That is because there is so much evil on the Earth now and it will infect *Ina Maka* even more in the coming time. Just like a sickness can quickly take over a body, so can evil quickly take over a planet. This evil has kept humankind from making true spiritual progress, and it will get worse and worse as the new era approaches.

"There is goodness on the Earth, as well as evil. Humans have free will. People can choose the good, turn away from evil, and move entirely toward love, peace, compassion, and higher spiritual learning. There are many people on the Earth who have done this. Your Grandmother is a good example, and now she's teaching you to go forward in this way.

"The coming time will be very difficult. Many more humans will turn to evil, and this phenomenon will be seen across the planet. Evil will convince massive numbers of people to hurt others, and cause all to sink into a state of spiritual darkness and hopelessness. A ruthless few will rule the Earth planet through complete cruelty and fear. They will control all the money and will greedily become richer and richer as most of the population becomes poorer and poorer.

"*Wakan Tanka* will not allow evil to take over His entire planet. He will finally end evil's massive influence and help rid the Earth of all evil. This is the promise He is making to all who can see and hear Him."

The *Ogligle Wakan* became somber and subdued for an instant. The other angels around us began singing a beautiful song. The quiet reassurance of their exquisite voices reached us and lifted our spirits.

"*Zintkala Zi Win*," he continued. "Evil is not a natural part of God's creation. It came here long ago and established itself. Humans add to its power when they turn away from *Wakan Tanka* and are then left open and unprotected. Evil knows how to quickly move in with its infections.

"People on Earth think that good and evil are opposites, but they are not. *Wakan Tanka* created the world with sets of opposites, but evil is not part of that creation. Good is a state of being that is loving, and evil is the absence of this state, not its opposite.

"Evil wants power. It knows it can manifest what it wants and so it does. It creates power over others and thus more power for itself. It wants to control others for its own use. It does not want to allow others to be free to love and learn. Evil fears the advancement of humans toward the good because it fears people will become stronger than itself. Evil beings are very fearful even though they appear to be powerful.

"When evil is present in any form, it will always try to get power over a person or groups of people. When it does get power, evil feels less fear. Unfortunately, evil feeds on itself. The more powerful evil becomes, the more it fears it might lose its power. This is when it becomes even more dangerous, because it keeps trying to get increasingly more power. As evil manifests more and more evil, it gets darker and darker and can cause horrendous outcomes.

"In the coming time, evil on Earth will become very strong and exceedingly difficult to defeat. Evil will try to destroy *Ina Maka* and force the planet into its own manifestation of total evil. If that were to happen, *Wakan Tanka's* beautiful creation of the planet Earth would be forever destroyed and evil would have total power and control.

"The Creator will not allow this to happen. *Wakan Tanka* will send legions of *Ogligle Wakan* to Earth. They will be the warriors to defeat evil and make certain that it is eradicated from the planet Earth."

Upon hearing these words, the *Ogligle Wakan* who surrounded us proudly raised their heads higher as if they were already preparing for battle.

"*Wakan Tanka* will send legions of *Ogligle Wakan* to fight and destroy evil. Never has the Creator sent so many to battle evil. As a result, there will be a celestial war never seen before with scores of unimaginable battles.

"The legions of *Ogligle Wakan* will be escorted by millions of *Wanbli Gleska* into the earthly plane. Humankind will see the masses of flying eagles, but will not see the Angels. The coming of the *Ogligle Wakan* will be so magnificent it will be as if Heaven and Earth were connected by a giant pathway in the sky. Before each battle, brilliant lights will be seen and beautiful voices singing sacred songs will be heard. Some people will see and hear them, but most will not. All humankind will be witnesses in one way or another to the celestial battles as they rage on endlessly. Eventually all evil will be destroyed.

"Once the destruction is complete, the *Ogligle Wakan* will prepare the way for *Ptesan Win* and the Benevolent Ones to descend upon the Earth and establish love, peace, compassion, and a new way of living."

The *Ogligle Wakan* paused as he felt my distress. The vision of evil taking over our beautiful *Ina Maka* had overwhelmed me. Even though I knew *Wakan Tanka* would take care of everything in the end, I was sad to think about all the suffering and horror that would develop in the meantime. I was honored to be shown the visions, but in some ways, it was hard to see the visions of the coming terror they were showing me.

"Is there no other way for humans?" I asked with great respect, holding my gaze to the ground.

"Perhaps there will be another way," replied the *Ogligle Wakan* very gently. "Only *Wakan Tanka* knows the answer. But the Earth is now on a path with the total destruction of evil as the only possible outcome.

"You are young, and we honor your feelings of compassion for others. It is a very admirable place for you to be as a beginning medicine woman. You will be rewarded in Heaven based on your kindness. Envision the Earth that *Wakan Tanka* will establish and keep your mind off the destruction that is necessary before the new era can manifest.

"Many spirits, each from their own perspective, are showing you the same vision from *Wakan Tanka* of the coming time. The Benevolent Ones, the animal spirits, and the bird spirits all have a different assignment when the time comes. You will also have an assignment. Pay careful attention to all the signs you will see. Act on the directions you are given. Never doubt or ask questions when instructions come from *Wakan Tanka*."

"*Waste*," I replied.

"We will leave you now," the *Ogligle Wakan* said softly. "Keep these visions in your heart and soul. *Zintkala Zi Win*, never forget one detail of them."

"I will forever keep them in my heart and soul," I promised.

The *Ogligle Wakan* broke into a beautiful sacred song. They beamed blessings upon me and I once again felt at complete peace.

"*Wopila, wopila, wopila, wopila,*" I called to them gratefully as they continued in a celestial choir of beautiful songs. To be in the presence of radiant angel love and light was a wonderful uplifting experience beyond earthly words.

The *Ogligle Wakan* continued their loving singing. I listened and was held in rapture as the vision of them gently faded away and their eternal blessings were safely stored within me.

24

WARRIOR ANGELS

God's mightiest
Fighters of evil
Led to Earth
By legions of Eagles
I pray they possess
The greatest strength
Courage and fortitude
Wisdom and knowing
Ate' Wakan Tanka
Hear my simple prayers
For the Angel Warriors
When the battles end
May they return
To your Heavens
In their complete glory
I pray for them
Humbly from my heart
And my deepest soul.

I sat in quiet for a time. The sun had moved to the West. I watched little white clouds float above me. I thought about everything I had seen on this, the second day of my *Hanbleceya*.

I was watching a cloud slowly move across the sky when I saw a very large *Wanbli Gleska*. He was golden brown and had a vast wing span. He hovered and circled over me for what seemed a long time. I felt joy and peace fill my heart and I realized he was beaming love down to me.

The *Wanbli Gleska* landed beside me. I realized he was bringing the next part of the vision. He told me I was to come with him. He asked me to climb on his back. I did as he asked, and we immediately flew upwards into the clear blue that was the sky.

He asked me to become an eagle like him, and I saw myself quickly change into a *Wanbli Gleska*. We flew together and caught up with other *Wanbli Gleska* and formed a flock. We flew higher and higher to the outer perimeters of the atmosphere.

"We're going on a mission to escort the *Ogligle Wakan* to Earth," the *Wanbli Gleska* explained. "This is one of our daily duties. We're always ready and standing by."

Unci had taught me that the *Ogligle Wakan* came to Earth often. Some *Ogligle Wakan* escorted new souls to be born and some escorted souls who had lived on Earth and were leaving their bodies.

The *Wanbli Gleska* knew they would escort the *Ogligle Wakan* in great masses to the Earth in a coming time. It was predicted in the skies. The *Ogligle Wakan* would come down with certain alignments of the Heavens and they would call the *Wanbli Gleska* to come help them.

Using the eagle medicine was something I'd been trained to do by *Unci*. I could go to the *Wanbli Gleska* and ask for their help to heal someone, or for spiritual guidance, or for a vision to help a situation. I was also learning how to ask the *Wanbli Gleska* to help me get rid of a bad spirit in someone. They knew how to take it away from the Earth and get rid of it.

I continued flying with the brown *Wanbli Gleska* to the edge of the outer skies where we joined up with other *wanbli*. There was much excitement among them. The *Wanbli Gleska* told me they had seen the time when legions of *Ogligle Wakan* would come to Earth to help *Ina Maka* and humankind.

The *Wanbli Gleska* then showed me the future and what their assignment would be.

"*Zintkala Zi Win*," he called out my name. "In the coming time, legions of *Ogligle Wakan* will come to Earth. This has been prophesied by our people for a long, long time. The *Wanbli Gleska* know their help will be needed when legions and legions of *Ogligle Wakan* will come to rid the Earth of evil."

Suddenly, I saw the outer skies filled with *Ogligle Wakan* flying toward Earth. They came through the vibration of light and sound. They were translucent and beautiful with white bodies, white auras, and white translucent robes.

The sound they made took my breath away. They sang sacred songs in a beautiful chorus of voices mixed with celestial echoes. They were wonderful, awe inspiring, and transfixing.

The *Wanbli Gleska* were very honored to escort the Angel Spirits. They were the eyes for the Angels as they entered the earthly realm from the Heavens and the Eagles helped them make the transition.

As we neared the Earth's outer atmosphere, the *Wanbli Gleska* lined up, hovering in the skies, and the *Ogligle Wakan* lined up behind them. We waited until all had gathered. There were so many legions of *Ogligle Wakan* that I couldn't see where they began or ended.

When the formations were in place, the Chief of the *Ogligle Wakan* blew a large flute, which made the most beautiful sounds and at the same time sent massive vibrations downwards to Earth. To us in the skies, the vibrations felt like waves of goodness rolling over our very beings.

The *Ogligle Wakan* broke into numerous harmonious sacred songs, which sent beautiful vibrations and further waves of sound. As they sang, they simultaneously sent brilliant rays of vibrant colors downward toward Earth. I listened and watched, and was transfixed by the beauty and wonder of what I was seeing and feeling. I didn't want it to end, so great was its power. I wanted to stay and be in the state of angelic bliss forever.

I don't know how long the *Ogligle Wakan* sang and sent rays of colors to the Earth, but it was a long time. When they were finally ready, they asked the *Wanbli Gleska* to guide them to Earth. The *Wanbli Gleska* led the descent from the outer ether and the *Ogligle Wakan* continued their singing as the legions of Eagles and Angels entered Earth's atmosphere.

It was early, early dawn in the vision when the *Wanbli Gleska* and the *Ogligle Wakan* first arrived in the skies. Earth was just awakening to a new day. The animals and birds were the earliest to see the celestial sight. Most *wamakaskan* (animals) stood still and watched in amazement. The *zintkala* (birds) broke into song and then quickly flew in all directions to get out of the way. The *tatanka* (buffalo) herds stood very still and reverently raised their heads toward the skies. The *tahca oyate* (deer people), *hehaka oyate* (elk people), and *sunkawakan oyate* (horse people) reverently watched.

Some humans stopped and stared, but most did not. Only a few could see the masses of *Wanbli Gleska* descending, and they were awed. Others could feel something wonderful and suddenly felt very blessed. A very, very few could see the *Ogligle Wakan* descending behind the Eagles, and they stopped everything they were doing and watched in exaltation.

The *Ogligle Wakan* arrived in the skies of the planet Earth to do battle with the evil ones. As evil was roused by the great presence of the Angels, it trembled violently in fear and frantically tried to hide. The *Ogligle Wakan* saw the evil no matter where it tried to hide or what creature it tried to inhabit.

The Angels used massive sound vibrations and intense color rays to blast evil out of various kinds of bodies. Evil was immediately forced out of its hiding places. It fought back viciously and horrendously and directly attacked the *Ogligle Wakan*. The fighting was fierce and grotesque. It went on and on until I was sickened by the sight of the battle I was witnessing.

As instructed, the *Wanbli Gleska* took the evil entities to other *Ogligle Wakan* waiting outside Earth's atmosphere. The waiting Angels pulverized the evil entities with rays of fire and reduced them to nothingness.

As the battled raged on and intensified, terrified humans took shelter. Most people didn't realize what was really happening. They just knew that very unusual, massive storms were taking place across the planet. The *Wakiyan* flashed thousands and thousands of lightning bolts, far more than usual. Their loud rumblings, flashes, and storms provided cover for the celestial battle and kept people from seeing what was really happening.

The *Ogligle Wakan* took millions of evil entities from the Earth. The numbers were staggering. The Eagles, who helped the Angels, could not believe so much evil had been lurking and hiding on the planet.

Because of the immense battle, humans became terrified and very fearful as millions of people suddenly died for no apparent reason. Evil was so entrenched in some human beings that people would die instantly when the evil was suddenly removed. Masses of people fell ill and died very quickly. Great panic spread across the Earth. Animals also died suddenly in the same way as people.

Evil was forced out of *Ina Maka* as She also had become infected with humankind's negative ways.

The Eagles solemnly did their work as they had been instructed by the Angels. It was hard and emotionally draining. We all felt very sad and sorrowful for the humans and animals who were going through so much suffering. We knew it was necessary and appropriate, but we felt the weight of it just the same.

The *Wanbli Gleska* motioned for me to follow him. We flew back to *Paha Sapa* and my *Hanbleceya* site on *Mato Paha*. I found myself gently returned to my buffalo hide. He landed beside me and continued his instruction.

"The war against evil will not be over with one battle," he explained. "In the coming time, there will be many battles over a long period until every evil entity is taken from the Earth. Each battle will be like what you have been shown. The *Ogligle Wakan* will call the evil with intense sound and color. The evil will be tortured by it and will try to resist. Despite horrific fighting, the evil will be forced to leave the humans, animals, and lands that it has inhabited. Evil will eventually show itself every time the *Ogligle Wakan* call it into battle. It will be guided away and pulverized in the outer atmosphere.

"It will take immense fighting ability and enormous battles for the *Ogligle Wakan* to rid the Earth of evil. We *Wanbli Gleska* will help with the battles and do our part as instructed by *Wakan Tanka*. Never before have we been called to execute such profound duties. These will be the most terrifying battles we *Wanbli Gleska* will ever take part in. We are very honored to serve our Creator in this way when the time comes. We are very grateful that *Wakan Tanka* has boundless faith in us and will call on us to help. We are honored to serve Him."

The *Wanbli Gleska* flapped his vast wings and soared above me.

"*Wopila, wopila, wopila, wopila,*" I called out to him. "Thank you for taking me with you and giving me this great vision. I am very humbled."

He called back with a sound like a whistle and flew higher and higher until I could no longer see him. I now felt one with the *Wanbli Gleska,* and I knew he and the other Eagles would often be with me.

25

SACRED VISIONS

To be kept
Eternally
In my soul
So powerful
They transcend
Time and space
And lifetimes
Wakan Tanka
Guide me from
The blackness
To the light
From the illusory
To the genuine
That I may live
In your divine truth
Forever and ever.

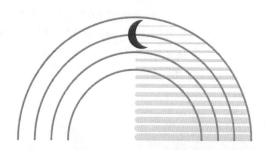

I felt peaceful and happy with my buffalo robe around me and thought about the vision the *Ogligle Wakan* and the *Wanbli Gleska* had shown me.

"How beautiful *Ina Maka* will be in the coming time," I thought to myself, gratefully memorizing each detail of the vision so I would never forget.

My attention shifted as I heard sudden loud noises coming from the West. Before I realized what was happening, the *Wakiyan* flashed energy into the ground around me. I could see a very black intense storm off in the distance. Its clouds were huge and frightening. As I watched, the storm whipped itself violently into dozens of tornadoes and the skies became dark as night.

The *Wakiyan* spoke. "*Zintkala Zi Win*, do not be afraid. The storm you're seeing is a vision. We want to show you what the storms will look like to people on the ground. You will better understand the duty we *Wakiyan* will have in the coming time when evil is destroyed."

Before I could take a breath, I saw the celestial battle between the *Ogligle Wakan* and evil. The Angels took the evil high into the skies and pulverized it in space. Below the fighting and on the ground, violent black storm clouds full of tornadoes, fierce lightning, and loud crashes of thunder were all that could be seen and heard.

The massive clouds poured down torrents of unending rain and pounding hail. I saw how the *Wakiyan* gave ground cover for the *Ogligle Wakan* who fought the battle against evil above the clouds.

The enormous storm brought all forms of life on Earth to a standstill. People sought places of refuge from the violent winds and could not navigate through the deep waters. The ferocious hail prevented people and animals from leaving their dwellings. The fierce lightning and downpours of rain made it easier for the *Ogligle Wakan* to find the evil and call it out of humans, animals, and lands.

I realized how frightening the storms would look to all living things on Earth. They would not be able to see the battles above the storm clouds to realize what was happening. The storms would feel excessive and unusually frightening to them. They would be terrified. The massive storms would strike again and again, each time causing widespread panic.

The *Wakiyan* spoke. "*Zintkala Zi Win*, the vision is showing you how we *Wakiyan* will be part of the battle strategy. Even though it will be difficult, we want to help. It is our duty and we are very dedicated to our mission. We have been exceedingly concerned to learn about the pollution of the skies and the illness of *Ina Maka* that will be manifested in the coming time. Evil will make the Earth Mother and the atmosphere of Father Sky gravely ill. The result will have enormously negative effects on the *Wakiyan*. We provide the energy Earth needs and the electrical charges that cause new growth and beginnings.

"If it were not for our love of *Ina Maka*, we would go away in the coming time. We don't have to stay on the planet. *Wakan Tanka* has given us permission to leave at any time. We feel it is our duty to stay for *Ina Maka* and fight evil when the time comes.

"We cherish you, *Zintkala Zi Win*, and your beloved *Unci*. You love us, honor us, and always pray to us to stay. That is why we work with you and your Grandmother as part of your medicine and help you with healings and seeing visions. We will continue to be there for you and to help you.

"We've shown you the *Wakiyan* duties in fighting evil when the great war begins in the time that is coming. Remember you will have a duty and be called upon to help as well."

"*Wopila, wopila, wopila, wopila*," I said humbly. "Thank you for showing me these visions and thank you for staying on Earth and helping *Ina Maka* and our people."

The *Wakiyan* flashed rhythmically in brilliant blues and whites as if in a dance with the eternal universe. They slowly retreated into the blackened sky full of furious storm clouds and churning winds.

I watched them in awe until I could no longer see them. The *Wakiyan* left me energized and hopeful and I longed to travel with them again.

As the setting sun opened back up in the skies and sent its blessings down on me, I felt at peace. I picked up my *Canunpa Wakan* and prayed for help to remember all aspects of the vision and to keep it deeply in my heart and soul. I vowed I would remember the vision forever as the dusk enfolded me.

26

MOLE PEOPLE

Sacred messengers

Of Mother Earth

Show me the truth

So hard to see

That I may

Fully understand

The Earth Mother's

Dire betrayal by others

And Her horrific suffering

In the time

That is to come.

The sun dimmed its rays into pinkish softness and the long shadows of evening appeared around me. The beautiful pine trees whistled as gentle breezes caught their swishing needles in song. *Paha Sapa* laid out before me bathed in the soft colors of a setting sun.

A *Wahinheya* (Mole) appeared from a hole not too far from me and jumped around trying to get my attention. Her behavior was delightful, and I smiled, giving her my full concentration. *Unci* had taught me that the *Wahinheya Oyate* (Mole People) brought messages from *Ina Maka*. I picked up my *Canunpa Wakan* and prayed to hear her message.

The little Mole settled down in front of me and became very quiet. I heard a low moaning as if someone were in great pain. I looked around but saw nothing. The moans intensified, and I realized it was someone in terrible agony.

The *Wahinheya* spoke. "It is *Ina Maka* you hear. She wishes to speak to you directly and show you a vision of Her suffering in the coming time."

I nodded and lowered my eyes realizing She would speak to me directly.

Ina Maka spoke in a voice that sounded weak and sickly.

"I am not the same. I cannot breathe as before. The air around me is dirty. Too many of the sun's rays strike my surface because the atmosphere is poisoned.

"My waters are polluted and diseased. Rivers carry my waters much like veins that carry blood in humans. Many of them are blocked by dams and cannot flow. Foul stagnation has infested them.

"My oceans are polluted. Just like much of a human being is made up of water, so am I, the Earth Mother. My physical waters have been hurt and threatened and I cannot adequately provide for all the species of fish, mammals, and plants that live in the ocean.

"My minerals are stolen from me. Humans think that digging for oil, coal, silver, and uranium has no effect on me and so they dig deeper and deeper. It does affect me terribly, and it alters what I can grow and how I provide for all life on the planet.

"Many of the Creator's creatures are dying. Entire species cannot survive. I am sad when a plant, animal, or bird can no longer exist. *Wakan Tanka* entrusted me to provide for life on Earth, and now the survival of all beings is threatened. I have tried to balance myself and have been successful many times in the past. But now I am losing the battle to provide all *Wakan Tanka's* creatures with the sustenance they need for survival.

"I feel sick often and don't have nearly the energy I once had. There are many times I feel like I'm slowly dying. *Zintkala Zi Win*, teach all humankind to pray that *Wakan Tanka* will help me, and restore me to vibrant health."

I felt overwhelmed by *Ina Maka's* anguish as She spoke. We *Lakota* honored Her in all our prayers and made every effort to live with Her universal laws in peace and harmony, never wanting to harm Her. She had showed me a vision of what would happen in the coming time. I wondered when such terrible occurrences would happen. I quickly corrected my thinking about the question of "when" as *Unci* had taught me to do. I instantly said a prayer to *Wakan Tanka* acknowledging only He would ever know the timing of such things.

I prayed a long time for *Ina Maka* until the little *Wahinheya* danced around me again and asked for my attention.

The small Mole spoke, "You will need to pray for *Ina Maka* all the days you walk on the planet. In a future time, there will be more prayer centers devoted to Her. The reciting of prayers and the singing of ancient songs will cause vibrations of healing for our Mother. The prayer centers will be critical for the survival of *Ina Maka*. Devotion to Her will slow down the destruction that is coming. She will need continuous prayer beginning now because of the immense suffering She will be asked to endure."

I couldn't hold back the tears. I wept. The vision of a future time of terrible suffering for our Earth Mother was shocking to me. I sat at *Mato Paha* looking over the beautiful majestic *Paha Sapa*. I could not imagine a time when *Ina Maka's* bounty would be so destroyed that She would have trouble providing for Her creatures. I wondered how humankind could possibly come to such devastation. *Ina Maka* was their Mother too. She was the Mother of all animals, plants, water, lands, and rocks. She was the Mother of everything on Earth and it was all alive. I wondered how humans could harm their own Mother and all life around them.

I turned to prayer because I could no longer think of such terrible destruction. I asked the Creator to help *Ina Maka* and all Her inhabitants before it was too late. I prayed a long time until the little Mole and I were almost in complete darkness. Only traces of dim light remained.

The *Wahinheya* continued to watch me as I prayed. When I finally finished, she made a few loving sounds and then scurried back to her small hole and disappeared.

I prayed holding my *Canunpa Wakan* the rest of the quiet, tranquil night. I carefully tucked all details of the visions that I had been shown over the last two days deeply into my soul. I prayed to *Wakan Tanka* through the night to help me understand all the revelations that I was shown, and for strength and courage to continue to see the future.

27

NOBLE DEER

Precious to me

As spirit guide

The kind animal

I most resemble

The quiet animal

That rescues me

The calm animal

That loves me

The tender animal

That is my protector

I humbly honor you

Help me to live with you

Between the occurred

And the envisioned

Eternally and forever.

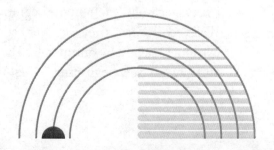

With the emergence of the sun's dawning light, I realized it was the beginning of my third day of *Hanbleceya*. The winds were quiet and peaceful. The hills of *Paha Sapa* came into view as daylight spread across the sky. It was still warm for December and I remained very grateful.

I heard snorting and hooves pounding. The noises came from the East and I looked in that direction. The early sunlight on the Eastern horizon blinded me from seeing anything but beautiful rays of orange light. The sound of pounding hooves continued until a form came into view.

A *Tahca* (Deer) unexpectedly appeared before me and reared on his hind legs. He had a full set of antlers and continued to snort and pound the ground with his hooves. A doe appeared right behind him and reared on her hind legs. They approached me in a manner that seemed urgent. I instantly knew I was to follow them and they would show me the next part of the vision.

My spirit ran after them, longing to go where they were going. I quickly turned into a *tahca*. We ran a very long distance and far away from my *Hanbleceya* site. More herds of *tahca* joined us.

We ran further and faster. The pounding of all the *tahca* hooves together gave us more energy to keep running. I felt elated and overjoyed to be included with the *tahca* herds.

We arrived at a high mountain in *Paha Sapa*. Many other *tahca* were waiting for us. I recognized some of them immediately. They were the powerful leaders of the *Wokcanka Tahca* (Deer Seers). *Unci* had carefully taught me beginning at a young age about the *Wokcanka Tahca*. They were very spiritual and considered to be extremely sacred by our people. They helped us in our healings and gave us new beginnings when we prayed to them.

One older female *Wokcanka Tahca* stepped forward and began to speak to all of us deer.

"*Wakan Tanka* tells us that we are to go higher to a special place. There will be shifts in the Earth and we will be safe in this high place. There will be plenty to eat and there will be water to drink. I've called you all here to inform you of the coming time.

"There will be great openings in the Earth as the Mother swallows that which cannot exist any longer. We are not to be afraid. We are one of the Mother's chosen creatures and She has led us to this place where we will be protected. We have all seen a beautiful time that is coming. *Ina Maka* will be very bountiful again. Her waters will run clean and all Her creatures will rejoice in Her wonder. The cleansing before the beautiful time will be hard, especially for humans. They will need our help and yet at times we must stay away from them.

"There will be a great cleansing of *Ina Maka*. We *Tahca Oyate* (Deer People) will be asked to help once the cleansing has been completed. Our responsibility will be to establish new beginnings on the Earth Planet. We will lead many creatures to experience love and peace again."

All who heard the *Wokcanka Tahca* speak were thrilled with Her words. We were going to be asked by *Wakan Tanka* to help *Ina Maka*. We loved our Creator and our Earth Mother. We would do everything we were asked to do. Our hearts were greatly lifted. We cheered and laughed, and our souls were filled with love.

The *Wokcanka Tahca* turned to me. "Remember this place, *Zintkala Zi Win*. You may come here often, especially for help with your healings. In the coming time, you will bring your people here and we will help them to survive."

Before I could reply, I found myself back on my special buffalo robe at my *Hanbleceya* site. I saw a *Wokcanka Tahca* walk away from me. I called out to Her, but then quickly realized I was back in my human body.

I sat with my *Canunpa Wakan* and prayed in gratitude for the vision I had just received. I again memorized the details so I would never forget.

The sun inched slightly higher in the sky and gave light to a wonderful new day.

28

DEER SEERS

Teach me

In the ways

Of your ancestors

How to pray

For Mother Earth

Deer Seers

I see you

I honor you

My heart

Weeps for our Mother

Deer Seers

Teach me

How to pray

For Mother Earth.

I sat peacefully on my buffalo hide. Cold little breezes caught my *Canli Wapahta* (tobacco ties or prayer ties) and I watched them dance in the late morning sun. The little bundles of cloth were connected to branches placed in the ground to form a square around me. I had made four hundred tobacco prayer ties while in deep prayer prior to my *Hanbleceya*. I watched the one hundred black ties that faced West twirl in the little gusts of wind, then the one hundred red ties that faced North, the one hundred yellow ties that faced East, and the one hundred white ties that faced South. I thought about all my prayers for a vision that the swaying *Canli Wapahta* symbolized. I smiled in appreciation, knowing that my prayers were being answered. The little cloth bundles waved happily in the wind as if in agreement.

Several *Wokcanka Tahca* suddenly appeared before me. They motioned for me to come quickly so they could show me another part of the vision. I was instantly up in the sky with them as we headed for the deep woods of *Paha Sapa*. In the higher altitude and in the vision, it was cold and snowing, yet I wasn't cold. I realized I was wearing a ceremonial dress like we wore at the sun dances, and not the leathers and high moccasins of my vision quest.

As we flew deeper and deeper into the woods I saw a tipi with smoke coming out of it. We were greeted by many *Wokcanka Tahca* as we landed near the tipi. The Deer Spirits led me into the tipi where several *Tahca Oyate* were waiting. I knew instantly that they had prepared themselves for a very sacred ceremony and I fell into silence out of humility and honor.

The *Wokcanka Tahca* took me back outside to an *Inipi* (Sweat Lodge). We entered the *Inipi* and the Deer Seer poured water on the hot rocks. He prayed deeply and told me we were doing a special ceremony for the Earth Mother after the Sweat Lodge. He quietly told me to watch how to conduct the special ceremony so that I could guide others in the coming time. I was very grateful and prayed that I would be worthy of such an honor. Once we had opened the doors of the Sweat Lodge four times, had said our prayers, and had smoked the *Canunpa Wakan*, we crawled out of the *Inipi*. I was given a dry ceremonial dress to wear. In the vision, I realized the sky was very dark and it was probably the middle of the night.

The *Wokcanka Tahca* led me back to the tipi and we entered together. It was pitch black inside. I could feel several *tahca* waiting for us to start. He began the ceremony by asking *Wakan Tanka* for His blessing.

The Deer Seer led us in prayer for new beginnings for *Ina Maka*. We prayed that She would be restored to Her original beauty in the coming time. We prayed Her waters would flow clean again. We prayed Her minerals and gems would be returned to Her. We prayed Her atmosphere would be cleaned and restored to its original perfection. We prayed that all evil would be removed from Her forever.

I prayed regarding everything I had seen in my vision. I prayed for Her to overcome all difficulties. I prayed that the removal of evil from Her would be quick and She wouldn't have to suffer a long time. I prayed that all creatures who lived with Her would return to love and respect for Her. I prayed humankind would never again harm Her.

The ceremony lasted many hours. The *Wokcanka Tahca* reverently prayed for their Earth Mother. They humbly asked *Wakan Tanka* to spare Her suffering and to help humans to understand the destruction they were causing. They prayed for the swift removal of evil from the planet. They prayed for a beautiful restoration of *Ina Maka* in the divine Creator's vision that would be even more wonderful than before the destruction.

The *Wokcanka Tahca* led us in a special prayer. He instructed us to use the prayer whenever we were praying for Mother Earth and during the special ceremony for Her.

> We raise our voices
> For Mother Earth
> We raise our hopes
> For Mother Earth
> We raise our prayers
> For Mother Earth
> We praise you, Mother
> We love you, Mother
> Be abundant
> Be balanced
> Be wild
> Be free
> Oh, Earth Mother
> Restore yourself
> We raise our voices
> For Mother Earth
> We raise our hopes
> For Mother Earth
> We raise our prayers
> For Mother Earth
> Dear Creator
> Help our Mother.

The *Wokcanka Tahca* reverently prayed this prayer and all the other *tahca* followed. They prayed fervently from their souls. The special ceremony came to an end and we said *wopila* prayers to *Wakan Tanka* and all the spirits who had guided us through the ceremony.

The *Wokcanka Tahca* led me out of the tipi. Soft light from an enormous full moon flooded my eyes and illuminated everything around us. The moon felt special and magical.

The Deer Seer took me to a little area where a large feast had been prepared in the tradition of thankfulness. We feasted with joyful hearts and rejoiced for we had all been shown a coming time of great healing and restoration for our cherished *Ina Maka*.

The *Wokcanka Tahca* gestured for me to follow him. As I walked toward him I found myself flying in the air. We flew back to the place of my *Hanbleceya* on *Mato Paha*. I was gently placed back on my buffalo hide. I looked around and realized it was daylight and not nighttime as in my vision. The sun was directly overhead and shone brightly all around the mountain.

"Remember, *Zintkala Zi Win*," the head *Wokcanka Tahca* spoke. "Prayers do not vanish after they are requested. Your prayers and the ceremony you just finished for *Ina Maka* will always be remembered, even in the future time."

"*Waste*'," I replied.

"Remember, too, that we *Wokcanka Tahca* will help you with new beginnings. *Tahca* spirits take seers like you to the future where they can see what will happen, or what medicine to use and how to use it to help someone. Both in healings and formal ceremonies, the *Tahca* spirits will help you and take you places that you cannot imagine in your young life right now.

"We have been with you from the time you were born. We have run with you and watched as you played. You have felt us as you hiked, climbed the rock cliffs, or gathered medicines with your *Unci*. You've especially felt us in the *Paha Sapa* because the *Tahca* are plentiful there.

"We have been with you your entire life and will continue to be with you, because we are your sacred animal. You have never lived in a place without the *tahca* spirits. We've always been with you. You've loved the *tahca* because deep down you've known we were your sacred animal. You look like a *tahca* and have *tahca* qualities. You are gentle, peaceful, and loving. You are also very quick and can run fast. You're athletic and agile. You have great strength like the *tahca*. You can stop, stand your ground, and charge if you must. *Tahca* are animals of the Earth that can fly in visions just like you do.

"The *Wokcanka Tahca* have taken you to the future that is coming. We have taught you during the special ceremony for the healing of *Ina Maka*. We've shown you the prayers to make for Her and the ceremonies to do for Her. We've revealed what *Ina Maka* will be like during the cleansing and the great change. We will also show you what She will be like after Her healing."

I thanked the head *Wokcanka Tahca* with my heart and soul and cried out, "*Wopila, wopila, wopila, wopila.*"

"All the *Tahca Oyate* (Deer People) love you, *Zintkala Zi Win*. When times get difficult, call us. We are always with you. We love you more than you have yet learned to love yourself."

29

SOULFUL PRAYER

The dutiful answer
In the coming time
Not to be victims
Not to do evil
But to pray
For our Earth Mother
All blessed life
And ourselves
To pray together
For the New Earth
That will manifest
Clearly as we
Pray.

The head *Wokcanka Tahca* stayed with me and rested quietly for a time to let me see the vision more clearly.

"See the mighty celestial battles in the distance," he exclaimed, breaking the silence, beginning another part of the vision.

I looked and saw fighting and storms far off in the distance.

"In the coming time," he explained, "whenever there is another battle, we will do special prayers. We will pray for *Ina Maka* and ask that She and all life can survive the horrible battles, and that all evil will be removed from Her and Her creatures on Earth. We will conduct special ceremonies just like the one we showed you."

The *Wokcanka Tahca* further explained. "We have overseen ceremonies for Mother Earth in the ancient way since the beginning of time. We learned from our ancestors that the Mother Earth and Her inhabitants needed spiritual and divine help. We *Wokcanka Tahca* came as *Wakan Tanka's* helpers. We brought medicine. From the beginning, we knew divine help was there when we prayed, and when we truly believed the burdens of the suffering planet, person, or situation would be taken away.

"We will perform Mother Earth's Ceremony each time a celestial battle occurs in the coming time. Our *Wokcanka Tahca* will conduct the ceremony with all the *tahca*. We will pray that She will be healed and restored. We will continuously pray that evil will not overcome Her. All medicine people will be asked to do the same. You will also pray very diligently during Ceremonies for *Ina Maka*.

"If the celestial battles are not won, evil will gradually take over every living creature on Earth including *Ina Maka* herself.

If evil captures the planet in the coming time, it will be very difficult to fight against it in the future. That is why the coming celestial war is so important. Good must win and evil must be gone from *Ina Maka*. An earthly kingdom of peace, love, and learning will need to be established.

"Earth was created by the Creator to be a special planet of great beauty and wisdom for *Wakan Tanka's* many creatures. Evil will have infected Earth so greatly the planet Herself will be in peril of being lost.

"The celestial wars will be very frightening and very difficult for people on Earth. Each battle will last days and days. With each battle will come huge storms so fierce that all life will be forced to stop and take shelter. It will be impossible to work or assume a regular life. People and animals will be forced to stay in special, reinforced shelters.

"We *Wokcanka Tahca* know *Wakan Tanka* will win, and so we will be patient. Much of humankind will not have the depth of faith needed and will be driven insane. The celestial battles will be very disruptive to peoples' existence on Earth. Many situations will be out of human control. People will go from awe to fear and then to hopelessness as the celestial war rages for an undetermined period.

"In time, life as humans have known it will change greatly. Evil will come out of hiding to do battle and will form brigades to fight the mighty armies from *Wakan Tanka*. As a result, there will be more lawlessness. Humans will turn against other humans. There will be more roving gangs who kill and plunder. There will be more armies of men with no national allegiance who will kill and wreak havoc on innocent people.

"The coming time will also focus on the good as the *Ogligle Wakan* do battles in the skies and reflect their goodness to Earth. People will come together. They will pray for each other and try to help. Much of humankind will be more giving and loving. The coming time of peace, love, and learning will be sensed by many on the planet Earth.

"*Zintkala Zi Win*, when it is time for the great cleansing, you will build a prayer center for your people. The dwellings will be round like tipis so that all who enter to pray can form the circle of life. We will show you how to build the dwellings. There will be sweat lodges, vision quests, and sun dances on the land. Even you will be amazed to see how beautiful and powerful a prayer center can be.

"You will be older or living another lifetime when the future events approach. You will have many people who will help you and be guided by you. It will be a difficult time for your people but also a hopeful time.

"Hold these visions in your heart. Know what is to come, but do not wonder the timing. Only *Wakan Tanka* knows. Remember we *Wokcanka Tahca* are always with you and will forever help you."

30

TAHCA TAUGHT ME
When visions
Come from God
Pray for compassion
And tolerance
Never judge
From a doubtful
Human view
Wakan Tanka
Help me embrace
Compassion
Help me remain
Humble and gentle
Help me walk
Waste' on your Earth.

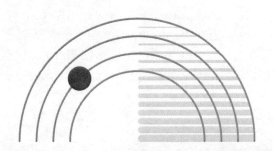

I thanked the head *Wokcanka Tahca* and told him how much I appreciated the lessons he and all the *tahca* had given me. It was true I identified a great deal with the *tahca*. I loved all the animals, birds, and plant spirits that came to me. When *Unci* told me the deer was my spirit animal, she pointed out the similarities both physically and mentally between me and the deer. I learned to have a special place in my heart for the *Tahca Wakan* (Sacred Deer) and often saw their spirits around me. When I was a young child they played with me, and as an older child, they accompanied me in daily life. *Unci* taught me how to ask them for help with healings or answers to difficulties as I studied to be a medicine woman.

The head *Wokcanka Tahca* stayed with me on my *Hanbleceya* site and we quietly enjoyed the sunshine and the peaceful moments. He silently helped me remember all that I had been shown regarding the Ceremony and Prayer for Mother Earth. I placed each instruction deep within my soul so I would never forget.

We both looked across the vast plains which stretched out to the North of us and were very visible from our vantage point on *Mato Paha*. The beautiful *Paha Sapa* rose majestically to the South. Bear Butte Mountain was uniquely positioned as the gateway to the hills from the North. We saw numerous *Wanbli Gleska* fly high above us, enjoying the afternoon sun and the uplifting breezes. The position of the sacred mountain and the beginning of the Black Hills surrounded by plains gave an exceptional pathway for the four winds to dance one at a time, and then in perfect unison.

The head *Wokcanka Tahca* and I saw the storm clouds gather in the West at the same time. We watched it and wondered where it would go. It quickly formed into a gigantic explosion of thunder with frightening flashes of lightning. We knew instantly that it was one of the celestial battles brewing in the Western skies.

"Look, *Zintkala Zi Win*," the *Wokcanka Tahca* shouted over the claps and booms we now heard, "A great *Wanbli Gleska* is coming for you." He pointed upwards to the part of the sky that was still blue.

"I see him," I shouted back.

"Go with him," he told me urgently. "He has important lessons for you. I will be with you later."

As I was expressing my gratitude to the *Wokcanka Tahca*, the *Wanbli Gleska* swooped down and landed right in front of us. I knew to climb on his back and let him take me where I needed to go. We flew toward the storm and the celestial battle which I could now see in full view. We kept our distance from the fighting, but still had a view of the battle happening in front of us.

The *Ogligle Wakan* drove their weapons of intense vibrations down to the Earth in bullets of hail. Next, they launched powerful light rays of dark color resembling that of evil, and they deeply pulverized the ground below.

The evil ones quickly left their inhabited victims on Earth in droves. They could not resist the angelic weapons and were enticed into showing themselves immediately. Evil responded with extreme anger and hatred and vowed to fight the *Ogligle Wakan* to death and drive them away from the planet.

The battle was ferocious and brutal. The warrior *Ogligle Wakan* appeared in forms of white light, which bounced off them and trailed them as they darted and gallantly fought above the storm. The evil showed itself on the ground in shades of dark colors that were absent of light. Their forms were distorted, hideous, and ugly. The evil ones made piercing ghastly shrieks that were so deafening it frightened us to our core. As the battle raged, the *Ogligle Wakan* demanded that more evil come out of their hiding places. The Angels sent their intense powerful weapons to force the evil ones to show themselves. Wave after wave of evil demons and hideous creatures came out of their hiding places. They were so insulted by the Angels they lost all realization and vowed to cause vast destruction of the Earth Mother to get even with the Angels.

The *Wanbli Gleska* realized that I was seeing evil. He quickly told me to erase it from my mind.

"*Wakan Tanka* wanted you to see the battle and the evil, otherwise you would not have been allowed to see it. When demons and all evil are in bodies or different places on Earth, they cannot be seen. They hide because that is their nature. *Wakan Tanka* wanted you to see and know what evil really looks like. He now wants you to erase it from your mind. No evil images are to be written on your soul in any manner. You do not need to carry it within you. Anything you need to see to help people will be shown to you, but only for the purpose of healing and helping. Otherwise you must never carry even the slightest image of evil. This is very important, *Zintkala Zi Win*, do you understand?"

"I do understand," I replied humbly. "I understand, and I will never hold images of evil in my heart or soul. I will pray for *Wakan Tanka* to show me whatever I need to know so that I may help, and then I will pray to remove the images from me forever."

"*Waste', lila waste',* (good, very good)" he replied, reassuring me.

My *Unci* trained me in the ways of the medicine women. Even as a young person, she taught me never to look at evil nor hear evil nor speak of evil. Sometimes I could see its forms when I helped *Unci* to heal people. She taught me never to really look at it or fixate on it. She repeated a phrase to me over and over. "See the evil in order to heal, yet don't see it." I practiced her teaching in everything I did. Not only would I not hold any vision of evil in my mind, I practiced never speaking of it, giving a detail of it, or pondering it in my mind. *Unci* taught me that holding onto any information of evil could actually call it to me.

She reminded me over and over to be very careful of its power and to practice the *waste'* way all my life and to forever walk the red road of the *Lakota*.

The *Ogligle Wakan* fought fiercely and aggressively. Many Angels were wounded as the battle stormed day after day. The *Wanbli Gleska* escorted the wounded Angels to places of healing down on the ground and new Angels took the places of the former Angels.

The *Wakiyan* gave ground cover for the battle by producing a storm so large and violent that it completely covered the battle from the ground. Below, the storm torrents of rain, exploding thunder, and blinding lightning terrified humans, animals, and birds.

Ina Maka shook violently with each massive ray of sound or color the *Ogligle Wakan* sent. The attacks were so ferocious they caused earthquakes and powerful shaking of the ground.

Time sped up for those of us watching the vision of the battle, and we saw day and night pass several times. The fighting continued. And then it abruptly stopped as we heard a loud sound and felt a wave of vibration from the *Ogligle Wakan*. This battle was over. We knew thousands of evil ones had been eliminated up in the skies. The numbers were staggering to us who thought evil had not gained that kind of infection on the planet. We believed this battle was over, but we knew the fighting would continue in another place. The Eagle told me the war wasn't over.

I climbed on the back of the *Wanbli Gleska,* and we flew a short distance to where we landed on a high ridge overlooking a beautiful valley. I recognized the ridge. It was only a few miles from Bear Butte Mountain where I still sat at my *Hanbleceya*. The valley below was the first one into the Black Hills from the North. My tribe had traveled along this ridge and into the valley many times.

The valley now looked very different. There was a large town of *wasicu* (white people) nestled among the hills of *Paha*

Sapa and extending out to the prairies on the West. I didn't recognize the dwellings. They were something I'd never seen before. Grandmother had told me the white men lived in square structures, so I thought this must be what she was describing. I wondered because there were so many structures, and some were very tall. Plus, the *wasicu* were not using horses. They climbed in shiny objects which took them places. I realized the town I was seeing must be sometime in the distant future.

As the *Wanbli Gleska* and I landed, a group of *Wokcanka Tahca* greeted us. The first one to run up and welcome us was the head *Wokcanka Tahca* who had so carefully instructed me. I slid off the *Wanbli Gleska's* back. I was happy to see the *Wokcanka Tahca* after witnessing the horrible battle.

We watched the people of the town from the high ridge. It was puzzling to us. There was so much activity with people going here and there. It seemed very busy and hurried. The sun was out and brightly shining on the town, making it easy for us to watch everything from the ridge above.

As we watched, clouds moved over us and blocked the sun. None of us high on the cliff or those down in the valley felt concerned or stopped what we were doing. The clouds were high and fluffy and seemed harmless even though they moved swiftly across the sky. The people below continued their work and we watched them with curiosity.

We all heard the *Wakiyan* at the same time. We were very surprised because they were suddenly right over us. We realized in an instant that it was another celestial battle. It passed over us so fast we didn't have a chance to react. We could hardly breathe.

The intense swirling storm clouds moved on top of the town and engulfed it. On our high perch, we watched as the *Ogligle Wakan* hurled their sound vibrations and war colors down on the town. Within minutes, the settlement fell apart and disintegrated.

The Earth shook violently, the structures were pulverized, and the town was no more. Everything was turned to dust. We heard the shrieks and horrible cries of evil as they were taken to the skies and destroyed.

I don't know how long the *Wanbli Gleska,* the *Wokcanka Tahca,* and I stayed on the ridge, too stunned to move. It rained in torrents over the battle site. We watched as the pounding water washed away any debris of the town until nothing remained.

The storm cleared. More *tahca* spirits ran to us to see if we were okay. The *tahca* continued giving information and I became quiet.

I didn't know how to feel after watching the destruction. The battle felt very personal, perhaps because it had been so close to us. The other battles I had witnessed were further in the distance and had not permeated my reality quite like this one.

We *Lakota* feared the *wasicu* because they continued to take our lands. We were especially concerned about them taking over our sacred *Paha Sapa,* where many of our medicines grew. Our chiefs tried to work with the chiefs of the *wasicu,* but it hadn't helped.

Unci taught me to pray to *Wakan Tanka* that our sacred *Paha Sapa* and our lands would not be taken from us. She taught me to pray for the *wasicu* and their families. *Unci* and I often made prayers for them and asked that they would open their hearts and settle in the vast lands to the West.

I was very concerned for the loss of life in the town that had been right below us. The head *Wokcanka Tahca* came to me and looked me in the eyes.

"It can be difficult to be a seer at times," he said quietly, trying to reassure me. "It's good that you have this compassion for others. Never lose it. You are young and will learn how to work with compassion for the good. Sometimes *Wakan Tanka* must show us all aspects of a healing so that we may better understand.

"He wanted you to see the extent of the evil that will be present on Mother Earth. He wanted you to see the destruction up close, so you would understand it. Never judge what He shows you. Always feel the compassion in your heart and soul and focus there. It will help you be a humble and very effective healer. Remember the healing you are being shown is for *Ina Maka*. Rest in your gift of compassion for Her."

"I will," I replied realizing the wisdom of his words. "*Wopila, wopila*. I am very grateful for your teachings and for helping me grow to become a more advanced healer."

The head *Wokcanka Tahca* asked the eagle and all the deer to form a circle. We joined him in prayer for *Ina Maka* and Her continued healing in the coming time.

31

THE CREATOR

Ever generous

Ever loving

Ever giving

To His Creation

The Creator

Wanting the best

Hoping for better

Walking *waste'*

For His Creation

The Creator

Patient in peril

Loving in helping

Giving in saving

His beautiful Creation.

The *Wanbli Gleska*, the *Wokcanka Tahca,* and I remained on the ridge. The terrible storm and celestial battle that had caused the destruction of the *wasicu* town had passed. I remained shaken by the destruction of the little village, even though I knew not to question the knowledge of *Wakan Tanka*. The *Wokcanka Tahca* made prayers for the wisdom of the Creator's ways. We prayed for the inhabitants of the town, for the new beginning for our Earth Mother, and for the ways of the Creator that were yet to materialize. We remained in deep prayer for *Ina Maka* for a long time as the vision continued.

As we finished our prayers, we saw beautiful lights in the sky. Flocks of *Wanbli Gleska* came into view, and we witnessed them leading hundreds of luminous moving lights. We watched in wonder as the eagles and the lights flew right over us and landed in the valley below where the town had once stood.

We stayed on the high ridge overlooking the valley. We watched quietly and in awe, not sure of what we were to do. None of us moved, so mesmerizing was the scene below.

We saw a few eagles land, but most of the hundreds of eagles remained circling above the lights, making it hard for us to see clearly what was taking place down in the valley. At first, we thought the eagles were just blocking our view and we strained to see what happened to the lights because they unexpectedly disappeared.

The *Wanbli Gleska* cried out in unison and flew around the valley in a massive circle. Their piercing sounds and the vibration of their wings made us stand in raptured attention. They flew around the valley four times and then landed in a vast circle while encircling hundreds of tall human-looking forms. The lights we first saw had vanished, and we realized the beings below us in the valley had come first as luminous lights flying in the sky.

The activity in the valley suddenly stopped. The eagles became very quiet as did the tall human forms. All movement stopped, and a peaceful silence fell over the land. It was then we first could see the tall forms much more clearly. We stopped breathing at the same time as we realized they were *Ogligle Wakan*. They didn't look like the warrior angels, and we wondered who they were. They were very tall with radiant white light around them, mixed with blue. They had the form of humans but were thinner than the warrior angels we had seen before. They were very agile and quick in their movements and displayed great physical grace.

One of the angels broke into song and led the others in a sacred melody. Their voices reached us on the high ridge. They sang in a language we had never heard but it did not need interpretation. It was so magnificent and sacred that we were moved to tears in loving appreciation until the singing stopped.

The head *Wokcanka Tahca* excitedly broke the silence. "I know the *Ogligle Wakan* who leads the singing. He is called the *Itacan* (Leader) and he has appeared to many of the Deer Seers. I feel it is important that we immediately go down and greet him and the angels."

We instantly agreed and formed a circle for prayer. We asked *Wakan Tanka* to bless us and to be with us as we went down in the valley to greet the angels and the eagles.

The *Wokcanka Tahca* spontaneously ran down the ridge to greet the Leader and we eagerly followed.

"*Itacan*," he called happily. "You have come!"

"Yes," he called out. "*Wakan Tanka* has asked us to come help Planet Earth and we are honored to be here."

We surrounded him with greetings of great warmth.

The Leader had a human form, but he was much taller than I realized from the ridge. Beautiful white light surrounded him with some blue-like lightning. I did not stare directly at his eyes out of respect, as *Unci* had always instructed me. He was excited to talk with the *Wokcanka Tahca,* and enthusiastically greeted them like old friends.

As I kept my gaze downward, I realized that many years had somehow passed because we all stood in high native grasses and the trees surrounding us were very mature. It seemed like the battle and destruction of the little town had just happened the day before, but I could see much time had passed.

"*Zintkala Zi Win,*" *Itacan* quietly called my name. "Look into my eyes. You have my permission."

I smiled in agreement and raised my eyes to meet his. I was immediately transported into the sky and everything felt wonderful around me. His eyes were black, and energy shot out of them in waves of wisdom and visions.

"*Zintkala Zi Win,*" he quietly spoke my name again. "Do not be afraid. I have appeared to your *Unci* many times. I am the Leader of the *Ogligle Wakan* who are the seers' clan. *Wakan Tanka* has asked us to help *Ina Maka* and all Her inhabitants by bringing the vision He has bestowed on us into reality. Because we can see His great vision, we are better able to carry it out and bring it into manifestation."

He held my gaze while giving me blessings of love, peace, and compassion. He touched my forehead and for an instant I saw the vision of the new manifestation of *Ina Maka* more completely than I had previously.

He brought me back down to the land with his gaze. "You will carry the ability of a seer, *Zintkala Zi Win,* all your days on the planet and into future lifetimes."

"*Waste*," I humbly uttered in appreciation. "*Wopila, wopila.*"

"There will be more, and I will continue to guide you. We are forever friends."

"*Wopila, wopila,*" I repeated.

He turned to the head *Wokcanka Tahca* and declared that we should partake of the large feast the Deer Seers had prepared for the Leader and his people. I grasped again that more time had passed than I knew, but so it was in visions. I saw the large feast waiting for us and appreciated that the *tahca* had gone back to their camp and brought needed supplies.

We feasted for hours, talking and laughing and getting better acquainted. The Deer Seers were like old friends to the Seer Angels and it seemed they hadn't seen each other in a long while.

The *Wokcanka Tahca* and *Itacan* people were very similar, even though they were in different forms. They both radiated joy. They laughed easily and expressed themselves in a cheerful, playful manner that made everyone at ease. I felt blessed, protected and healed just being in their presence.

Itacan and his angels explained in more detail why they had come to Earth. They said *Wakan Tanka* wanted them to help *Ina Maka* and teach humankind new ways of peace and love. They told us they would establish their headquarters in this valley. They said they wanted to build a large center of learning for all to use. They showed us their vision of the first building. I gasped when I saw it because it looked like a large crystal dwelling of beautiful translucence exactly as I had already been shown in the vision.

They told us they would name the new center *Mitakuye Oyasin,* which means "All My Relations" in *Lakota*. I felt this was a great honor, and I knew Grandmother would think so too. *Mitakuye Oyasin* was said in our ceremonies. It expressed our spirituality and how we felt about other humans, animals, and all living things. *Unci* taught me that we were one, all connected, and all respected and loved by *Wakan Tanka* and *Ina Maka*.

The *Wanbli Gleska,* the *Wokcanka Tahca,* and I spent the day and early evening with *Itacan* and his Seer Angels. It was a heavenly experience and one we would all forever hold in our hearts and souls. We felt love and peace. We laughed openly, and our hearts were filled with joy.

The head *Wokcanka Tahca* nudged me to follow him back up to the ridge. I was so much at peace that I felt nothing could ever disturb me again.

We happily flew back up to the ridge.

32

ANGEL SEERS
Far from home
Sent by *Wakan Tanka*
For Mother Earth
To move into a new era
One of light
Love and peace
Compassion
Forgiveness
Non-judgement
Inclusiveness
Tolerance
Angel Seers
Help us humans
On the Earth planet
Learn from you
To walk faithfully
In your love
And be forever free
In God's glory.

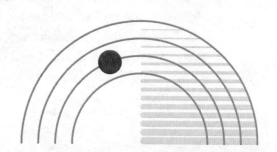

The *Wokcanka Tahca* and I flew back to my *Hanbleceya* spot on *Mato Paha*. I saw my body sitting quietly, still holding my *Canunpa Wakan* as I returned. I saw the head Deer Seer walk behind a few pine trees. He was gone, and I was left alone with my thoughts.

I looked around. I knew it was still the third day of my Vision Quest. Judging from the sun's position in the sky, I figured it must be afternoon. I reminded myself that earthly time, whether in days or years, was not recognizable in visions.

I went through all the details of what I had been shown, and carefully placed them in my heart and soul. I never wanted to forget.

I heard feet crunching on the ground and knew it was *Unci* approaching.

"*Apetu waste'* (good day), *Zintkala Zi Win*," Grandmother called as she came into view.

"*Apetu waste', Unci*," I called in reply.

"I've brought you sage tea, Granddaughter. The clouds say it will be a little colder tonight."

"*Pilamaya* (thank you) *Unci*."

I drank a few sips of sage tea. For a vision quest, we were given a little *pejuta* (medicine), but no food or water. The tea helped my parched lips and mouth and I was grateful.

"I am told you are having a very meaningful *Hanbleceya*. Tomorrow is your fourth and last day."

"I have seen so much, *Unci*, and have many things to ask you."

"*Waste'*," she replied and smiled. "*Waste'*."

"Will I see you in the morning?"

"*Hiya* (no)," she replied. "I will come to get you late in the evening before the sun starts to set. I'll take you down the hill and right into a hot sweat lodge. The *Inipi* ceremony will bring your *Hanbleceya* to an end. Remember to hold all that you've seen in your *cante* (heart), and guard it like the beautiful treasure that it is.

"*Han, Unci* (yes, Grandmother)," I said, smiling at her lovingly.

She gave me a big approving smile, turned, and walked back down the hill. I watched her disappear behind a little ridge and listened until I could no longer hear her.

I loved my *Unci* and appreciated the training she had so patiently given me in my young years. She taught me true compassion for people and I vowed as a little girl that I wanted to be just like her. Members of the tribe respected her, honored her, and held her in the highest appreciation. She was their doctor, their priest, and their counselor all in one. She was a humble spiritual being who gave her life to the people and put them above herself.

My thoughts drifted to the sounds of hooves crunching in the snow and soft snorting.

"Come with me, *Zintkala Zi Win*," the head *Wokcanka Tahca* said to me as he moved from behind the pine trees. "We will join the others. Another part of your vision is unfolding."

As I followed him, I turned into a *Wokcanka Tahca*. We ran down the hill at *Mato Paha,* then took flight and flew. I loved how the deer dashed across the land and then soared in the air. It gave me a feeling of freedom and joy.

We flew back to the high cliff overlooking the place where we had last seen *Itacan*. Several *Wokcanka Tahca* were already there and were watching what was happening in the valley below.

I cast my eyes down from the high cliff and into the valley. I quickly realized a long time had passed. It looked like *Itacan* and his angels had nearly finished the building of a new town they were naming *Mitakuye Oyasin* (All My Relatives). There were many more of the translucent structures already built and being used. They formed a large circle which took up the entire valley. The buildings in turn were encircled by the magnificent hills that looked like *tatanka* (buffalos). There were so many structures I didn't find the need to count them. I just soaked up the exquisiteness of the beautiful place the *Ogligle Wakan* had built.

All the structures were translucent. Each one was slightly different from the other one. Some dwellings were square with rounded edges and some were round. Some were tall, and some were short and more spread out. I had never seen dwellings of any kind on Earth that were so beautiful and magical.

As the sun's rays took turns illuminating some buildings and then others, we watched, fascinated. The sunlight made the structures glow, and colored rainbows reflected the rays back as the light reached them. The buildings were living, breathing entities that delighted in the sun's warmth and reflected their appreciation. The valley was filled with multicolor and beautiful tinkling sounds. It was a wondrous dance of light, heavenly echoes, rainbows, and the celebration of creation.

"Come, *Zintkala Zi Win*," the head *Wokcanka Tahca* softly said, nudging me.

As we walked slowly down to the valley, I returned to my human form. We saw shadows moving inside the structures, but we could not fully see them. We walked up to the first building we had been shown on our last visit. We entered through a doorway.

"Welcome," *Itacan* called to us.

Surrounding the Leader were many Angel Seers as well as animals and birds. The Angels were teaching them, and we could see that all species were highly honored with *Itacan* and his people.

"Join us," *Itacan* said, leading us to the center part of the building which was a large, round gathering place. Many of the Leader's people had already assembled. They warmly welcomed us. We were invited to sit on chairs which were also translucent like the buildings. We found them to be surprisingly strong.

The walls and outsides of the building were porous, letting in fresh air and sunshine. Since it was a beautiful spring day outside, the air was allowed inside. It felt like we were sitting in the open-air and yet we were in a structure. The fresh air reached my nostrils as if I were sitting by an open window. The sun beamed down on us and yet the sun's rays were somehow diffused as if we were sitting in the shade. The light refracted into rainbows on the inside of the building. I heard tiny sounds from the structures like musical notes and beautiful tinkling melodies as I waited for the lessons to begin.

The overall feeling of *Mitakuye Oyasin* was wondrous, peaceful, loving, hopeful, calming and joyful. I marveled at how the Leader and his people had built the heavenly structures.

Itacan began the lesson by welcoming the group. He told us that each one of us had a very important role to play in the new manifestation of the Earth Planet and we would all be taught by the Angel Seers. He said that humans would be trained last, when they were more prepared to receive such teachings. He showed us a large diagram of the town, *Mitakuye Oyasin,* and told us how each building had a specific teaching purpose.

He said the main building we were sitting in was for large gatherings. He showed us that all animal and bird species could come together in the large dwelling and that legions of humans would follow in time. He told us that each building had a specific purpose. One was designed to teach the new value system, one for spirituality, one for doctoring, one for music, one for writing, one for art, one for engineering, one for architecture, one for mathematics, one for the new justice system, and numerous other functions needed for the revival of *Ina Maka.*

I sat for many hours listening to *Itacan* and was mesmerized by the details of the new time that was to come. I knew the vision was startlingly different from the way Earth was now. I was amazed and grateful that *Wakan Tanka* would send the Angel Seers to Earth to help all peoples. I marveled at the beautiful new beginnings for *Ina Maka* that would manifest in the coming time.

I felt my heart and soul swell with new hope. I had seen the vision of *Wakan Tanka's* new ways for *Ina Maka.* The vision made my faith very strong and I knew I would forever be devoted to our beloved Creator.

The lessons from *Itacan* for the day came to an end. He wished us all great peace and love as we left the beautiful building.

33

WHEN HUMANS
Turn their backs
On others
And fill themselves
With selfishness
Then greed causes
A scar on the soul
A blackness
That infects the heart
A coldness
That chills all goodness
A turning away
Of empathy
A shut down
Of compassion
Resulting in
A call to evil
To enter
And so, it does.

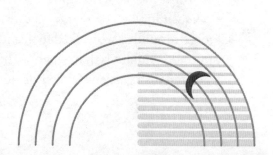

Several of the *Wokcanka Tahca* and I went back to the high cliffs overlooking the beautiful, lush valley with the translucent buildings twinkling down below us. The group rested. The Deer Seers were excited and inspired by *Itacan* and his Angels.

I felt very hopeful that *Ina Maka* would finally be set on a brilliant course of creation and renewal in the coming time. The village below us settled into a peaceful quiet. There was an air of anticipation in the wind.

Many hours passed. One of the *Wokcanka Tahca* excitedly called out to look toward the Eastern sky. I was spellbound as hundreds and hundreds of *Nagi Wakan* (Sacred Spirits) flew over us and landed on the edge of the valley. They formed a long line and waited patiently to enter the village. The *Nagi Wakan* had beautiful blue light around them. The color bounced toward the sky in a sea of vibrating blue as they stood together in a long procession.

The group of us descended from the high cliff to ask *Itacan* if we could help him with the huge numbers of visitors that were waiting. As we approached the main building, he came out and greeted us.

"I'm so happy you have come back. The *Nagi Wakan* are here to learn, worship, pray, and meditate. Would you, *Zintkala Zi Win*, and the *Wokcanka Tahca* help me welcome them?"

"*Waste', waste',*" we replied.

Itacan took us to a large gateway right outside the village. I looked around as we walked to it, and quickly realized there were now more buildings than when we had last visited. I saw massive trees and lush gardens with enormous flowers and plants. More *wamakaskan* (animals) were present, with each one having a duty to perform. It looked like years had passed, but I wasn't sure because vision time is far different than earthly time.

Itacan gave us specific instructions. We were to send each of the *Nagi Wakan* to different buildings. As they arrived, the *Nagi Wakan* were divided into various groups according to the subject they were sent to Earth to learn. *Itacan* and his Angel Seers taught advanced physics in one building, advanced mathematics in another, advanced music and vibration, advanced word manifestation in writing and speaking, advanced art and visioning, advanced spirituality, advanced communication with *Wakan Tanka*, advanced science. There were many more subjects, and each had its own building of learning. I had no knowledge of the subjects, but I knew they were necessary to manifest a new way for the Earth Mother.

The lessons were taught from the vision *Wakan Tanka* had given *Itacan* to bring *Ina Maka* back to Her original glory. *Itacan* had been assigned the task of leading the effort in all areas for the Earth Planet to be healed and restored.

The *Nagi Wakan* had once lived on the Earth as humans and their souls had risen to a very high level of love, peace, and compassion. They would take the education they learned at *Mitakuye Oyasin* back to their people around the world and teach them. In time, humans who currently lived on the planet would themselves come for further education to take back to the other humans they represented.

The Benevolent Ones, who inspired connection to *Wakan Tanka* throughout Earth's history like *Ptesan Win* and others, would lead the *Nagi Wakan* as they taught their respective people across the planet.

Itacan had given us a diagram with instructions, and we were able to help the *Nagi Wakan* to the building each one had been assigned. The dwellings of learning swiftly, yet leisurely, filled to capacity and we sighed in relief. All the *Nagi Wakan* were placed where they needed to be and were ready for their lessons.

Itacan joined us and told us we had done well with the *Nagi Wakan*. He asked us to follow him, and we were a little surprised. Everyone assumed he would be teaching. He led us to a grove of pine trees and asked us to sit down.

As if reading our minds, *Itacan* gently laughed and said, "I am going to teach today after all."

We responded with happy laughter, "*Waste', waste'*."

"*Zintkala Zi Win,*" he began. "It must be hard to accept the vision of destruction *Ina Maka* will go through because of humans. Your experience on Earth right now is living as one with *Ina Maka* and never destroying Her.

"Yes," I said quietly. "But I do believe in visions."

"*Lila waste'* (very good)," he replied. "We are pleased with your ability to see and accept visions and we all love you immensely."

I saw the *Wokcanka Tahca* nod and smile in agreement.

"I want to help you understand the way humans fall into evil. First, evil is present on Earth. In your time, *Zintkala Zi Win*, both good and evil are present on the Earth. Your *Unci* has taught you to stay connected to *Wakan Tanka* and carefully walk the balance between good and evil in every effort in your life."

I nodded in agreement.

"When humans cut themselves off emotionally from other humans, they are at risk. When humans forget that all creation is connected as one, they are at risk. When humans put themselves first and go down the path of selfishness, they are at risk. When humans achieve total selfishness followed by privilege, not only are they at risk, but they have crossed a universal barrier and are in danger.

"Many people never go beyond this point. They aren't taken over by actual evil, but they do get stuck in negativity. They may or may not stay connected to *Wakan Tanka* in worship and prayer. The Creator sees that many humans cause themselves suffering. He is patient and will forgive them and help them if they ask. Often, they do not ask because they do not realize what is happening to them. They become more and more influenced by the worldly negativity circulating around them, and their souls become more vulnerable to sliding into a worse situation.

"Evil has been on the Earth a long time. It has caused horrendous wars, plagues, jealousy over land, humankind attacking each other, family squabbles, diseases, accidents, and difficulties of numerous kinds. As you've been shown, evil will be destroyed in the coming time and *Wakan Tanka* will establish a new world on *Ina Maka*.

"Unfortunately, before the coming time, evil will become considerably stronger. Everything on Earth will be out of balance and the suffering will be extensive. *Wakan Tanka* will not allow His beautiful creation to be destroyed, and in the coming time He will act. This is the vision you've been shown.

"Evil overpowers a human when he or she decides they are better than others and no longer believe they are one with all living creation. This disconnection from others causes them to allow greed into their lives. They feel they deserve every desire they have but others do not. Greed feeds itself. The more humans allow greed the more they become malicious. Evil is attractive to some, and humans call it to them without realizing. Evil is happy to respond when invited. Humans then begin to display an emptiness of character and concern as evil invades. They are devoid of empathy and compassion. Kindness and consideration no longer have a place in their hearts. They are better, smarter, richer, and more entitled than other humans.

"The infected humans now do not identify with anything but evil. They quickly learn to disguise this part of themselves and find devious ways to pretend to be what they are not. As this process continues, evil takes them over steadily and silently. Soon, they are totally inhabited and under evil's complete direction.

"The suffering they cause to others is immense. Evil hides the damage they cause to themselves. They hide it so perfectly that humans may never be able to see the destruction of their own souls. Evil finally takes over the affected humans completely. Outwardly, humans display more clinging behavior, especially to material things, the amassing of fortunes, the destruction of others who get in their way, the planned manipulation and consequential demise of others, the constant and insistent lies to others, the total lack of responsibility for their actions, and the consistent blaming of others for their own mistakes.

"These are just a few of the many ways evil is displayed in peoples' behavior. Humans who are infected also have very little or no empathy or compassion. Evil disguises this fact very carefully. Infected humans can often appear to be empathetic and compassionate even though they are totally devoid of such feelings. Evil must hide itself, and it will take extraordinary steps to conceal itself while hiding in a human being and causing destruction."

Itacan stopped his lesson momentarily and sighed. "It's hard to hear about evil, isn't it?" We all agreed and hung our heads.

"We will switch to the good and the vision of the new Earth that is to come. I must caution you. It was necessary to teach you a little about evil, so you can better understand how it's possible for humans to become infected. Now release the thoughts to the sky. You must never hold on to notions, concepts, feelings, or any aspect of evil. Erase it from your minds. Don't feel sorry for the miserable suffering I have showed you. Don't think about it. Erase it now."

We lifted our heads and asked for help to release all aspects of evil.

"*Waste*," *Itacan* declared as he watched us send mental images of negativity and evil to the sky.

"Follow me," *Itacan* said as he started walking.

We followed him to a large garden where there were enormous plants and beautiful blooming flowers. We went to a large white flower. Its petals were longer and wider than me. *Itacan* put me in a meditative state and guided me to float above the impressive white flower. I felt a lovely force of love and healing arise in me. The white flower continued sending me goodness and healing as I remained floating in its restorative field of energy.

Itacan asked the white flower to release me. I found myself standing softly on the ground in a matter of seconds.

"Wonderful," I exclaimed, "Beautiful!"

"Come, come," *Itacan* called to us.

We walked down many rows of plants and *Itacan* explained each one of them to us. The plants and flowers towered above us. As we passed each one we felt gentle vibrations of love and peace being sent to us.

We reached the end of the garden and *Itacan* began to instruct us. "In the coming time, life on Earth will reach its full potential. Since love and peace will rule the planet, all life will be nurtured. Humans and all beings will give love and peace back to the planet because of first being given the planet's wonderful gifts. People and all creation will vibrate at a much higher level of existence. They will radiate goodness and light. People will become very advanced and make decisions based on the most loving way for all life on the planet. Because the Creator's love is expansive, all beings will create increasingly more love around them.

"The potential in each human will be unlimited in an existence of such peace and love on the future planet Earth. The good in all creation will create more and more good as the new life on *Ina Maka* continues. Imagine the potential if everyone is walking the way of *waste'*. What can the planet Earth accomplish? How far can it develop compassion and empathy? How much love and peace can it grow? What kind of new human will it produce? What will *Ina Maka* look like in time? We all know it will be wonderful and enlightening, and we wait with *Wakan Tanka* in anticipation."

The *Wokcanka Tahca* and I rejoiced as *Itacan* stopped and smiled at us. We had a glimpse of what the new *Ina Maka* would be in the future. It was a prophesy and a vision of great love and joy. A future view of a loving and devoted Creator who forever was dedicated to protecting His Creation and guiding it in the way of the good.

"Our Mother will be saved truly and forever no matter the difficulties," we expressed to each other in complete gratitude.

"Truly and forever," *Itacan* replied as he gently beamed white light down on us.

"Our Mother is saved!" we repeated over and over. "Our Mother is saved!"

I suddenly found myself back on my buffalo hide on the side of the mountain. In earthly time, it was the night of my third day. I fixed my eyes on the little stars blinking back at me from the sky. I prayed deeply that I would never forget the teachings from *Itacan*. And I thanked the leader of the Seer Angels over and over.

34

CREATION JOINS

With the Creator

Mother Earth

Father Sky

Animals join

With their hearts

Humble and devoted

To the Creator

Birds fly joyously

Through the air

In praise

Of their Creator

All creatures know

One with the Creator

Means worship

Of Mother Earth

I pray all humans

Join their souls

With love and devotion

To Mother Earth.

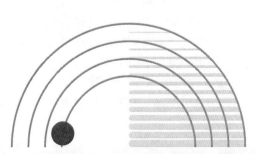

I opened my eyes and realized the sun was rising as it sent soft silhouettes of yellow light across the hills.

"My fourth day begins," I said to myself. "And what a glorious day it will be!"

A noise caught my attention and I looked in its direction. I couldn't see anything. I blinked several times trying to see. Within seconds, I was in another part of the vision.

I moved from my *Hanbleceya* place to the cliffs which overlooked *Mato Paha*. In the next instant, I saw *Mato Paha* erupt with blue light from Her inner core and out through Her volcanic cone. She sent plumes of blue light high into the sky. She emanated blue all around Her. As She shot continuous blue plumes upward, I felt tremendous vibrations with each powerful blast. The volcano-like emissions continued one after another in perfect rhythm and harmony.

I looked to the West and was amazed to see *Sunkawakan Oyate* (Horse People) gallop across the sky in such great numbers that the Western sky was darkened. The *Wakiyan* (Lightning Beings) followed the *Sunkawakan* and danced while flashing electricity as they approached *Mato Paha*.

From the North, I saw vast herds of *Tatanka Oyate* (Buffalo People) race through the sky. The herds were enormous and thunderous as their numbers swelled and moved toward the Mountain.

I saw the *Tahca Oyate* (Deer People) and *Hehaka Oyate* (Elk People) sprint from the East in great numbers. They flew through the sky gracefully and rapidly. They broke into singing as they neared *Mato Paha*.

From the South, I realized all the *Wamakaskan Oyate* (Animal People) that had four legs and the *Zintkala Oyate*

(Bird People) that had wings to fly charged toward the Mountain. Each sang their holiest song and soon came together as one harmonic chorus.

From the skies, the *Wanbli Oyate* (Eagle People) appeared. Their numbers were so many they appeared as clouds descending to the Mountain. Their piercing cries joined in the song all were singing.

Wahinheya Oyate (Mole People), *Tajuska Oyate* (Ant People) and all *Maka Oyate* (Earth People) quickly appeared from the ground. Their numbers were massive, and they formed rows of circles around the entire Mountain.

Suddenly, a huge *Wanbli Gleska* (Spotted Eagle) appeared and beckoned me to fly with Him. I threw myself on His back and we flew around *Mato Paha*. We looked down on all the *wamakaskan* and *zintkala* that had assembled as *Mato Paha* continued blasting Her blue plumes of light. The *Wanbli Gleska* told me the *wamakaskan* and *zintkala* had come for a blessing from *Ina Maka*.

I saw the *Sunkawakan Oyate* (Horse People) line up in rows on the West side of *Mato Paha*. Their numbers were huge. Hundreds of *sunkawakan* who were in the first row honored their Earth Mother by lowering their heads. They waited a few minutes in reverence, then turned and pranced to the back, letting those in the next long row come forward.

The *Tatanka Oyate*, who were first in a long row on the Northern slopes, also lowered their heads in reverence to the Mountain, and then moved back so the next row could come forward. They stretched beyond the horizon like a never-ending forest.

The *Tahca* and *Hehaka Oyate* (Deer and Elk People) lined up on the Eastern slopes in hundreds of rows that stretched beyond where any living creature could see. They too lowered their heads in reverence and then moved to the back in an orderly procedure.

The *Wamakaskan Oyate* with four legs and the *Zintkala Oyate* with wings lined up on the Southern side of the mountain in vast rows that stretched beyond the horizon. As they approached the front row, they too lowered their heads in reverence and then moved to the back of the line.

Hundreds of *Wanbli Oyate* lined up in wide circles in the skies around the mountain. There were so many eagles I couldn't see how high they went into the sky. The *Wanbli Oyate* nearest the mountain lowered their heads and then flew upwards and out of sight in the same procedure as the animals on the ground.

The *Wahinheya Oyate* (Mole People), *Tajuska Oyate* (Ant People) and all *Maka Oyate* (Earth People) followed the same pattern. They first circled the mountain's base, paid reverence to Her, and then let the next in line come forward.

The Great Blessing of Animals and Birds was breathtaking and held me and the *Wanbli Gleska* in complete awe. The movement of the *wamakaskan* and *zintkala* as they came forward and then moved to the next in line was done exactly at the same time in all six directions. As the *wamakaskan* and *zintkala* came forward, the blue light touched each one of them. *Ina Maka's* great blessing continued for days.

The *Wanbli Gleska* and I flew over the Great Blessing of Animals and Birds many times as the days continued. We saw no food nor water for them. They survived on the blue light of *Ina Maka's* blessings.

After all the *wamakaskan* and *zintkala* were blessed, silence fell. The animals and birds moved back slightly from the mountain and suddenly all activity stopped. There was no movement. The animals and birds waited. They waited longer. They continued to wait in silence.

The *Wanbli Gleska* and I flew back to the cliffs that overlooked the mountain, where we too could be silent for a time. We waited and waited. Nothing happened. It was as if all of us were suspended in time.

I was startled when the *Wakiyan* appeared from the West in blinding beauty and made their presence known in a way I had never seen before. They sang as they came toward *Mato Paha*.

The lightning danced across the sky and its thunder was more melodious. It did not touch the ground and it protected all the *wamakaskan* and *zintkala*. They were in prayer at *Mato Paha* and still stretched out for miles and miles beyond the horizon in all directions. None of them had left or strayed away from the mountain.

The *Wakiyan* thunder was rhythmic and the lightning sang. The *Wanbli Gleska* and I quickly realized we could hear their words.

> "We've come from Father Sky
> We've come from Father Sky
> Blessings we share for our Mother
> Blessings we share for our Mother
> And all who inhabit Her
> And all who inhabit Her
> We bless you
> We bless you
> We bless you
> We bless you
> We bless you
> We bless you."

The blessings were acknowledged in each of the six directions. As the blessings were sent to each group of the *wamakaskan* and the *zintkala*, they remained in reverent prayer.

The *Wakiyan* danced their way to *Mato Paha* and joined the blue plumes coming from the mountain's core in a magnificent show of joined energy. The *Wakiyan* united their charges with the volcanic eruptions from the mountain's core. The coming together of Mother Earth and Father Sky suddenly released new and stronger vibrations of blue energy. The Earth beneath shook and vibrated as the energy from Mother Earth and Father Sky swirled together in the intense blue light which danced all around the mountain.

The sound was deafening as the energies united and danced in praise of *Wakan Tanka* for His blessings to all. The *wamakaskan* and *zintkala* quietly remained in prayer.

The *Wanbli Gleska* and I sat on the trembling ground beneath us and remained in prayer. Instead of feeling fear, I felt complete happiness and rapture. I was moved to absolute gratitude, awe, and appreciation.

I realized that the *Wakiyan* came on the fourth day, in vision time, of the Great Animal and Bird Blessing. They danced the entire day and night. Their beauty was awesome and inspiring, and all stood still to watch them.

In the vision time of the fifth morning, they came with a very soft warm rain as the *Wakiyan* ordered clouds for all near *Mato Paha*. The animals awakened from their prayers and drank the precious water blessing from above. The *Wanbli Gleska* and I also drank.

As the *Wakiyan* stopped their dance, *Mato Paha* slowly and quietly stopped Her blue light emissions. The *wamakaskan* and *zintkala* drank the rain water blessing but still did not make any sounds. They sat in awe the entire fifth day and night. They sat in reverence and gratitude for the blessings they had received. They sat out of respect.

The rain clouds had moved to the East and the sun glowed in the early morning of the sixth day of vision time. The *wamakaskan* and *zintkala* remained in prayer still with no food and only the earlier rain water that had blessed them.

On the seventh day of vision time, we saw them move. They began the process of leaving to return to their homes. Slowly, and in very orderly fashion, they left *Mato Paha*.

The *Sunkawakan Oyate* left to the West, the *Tatanka Oyate* to the North, the *Tahca Oyate* and *Hehaka Oyate* to the East, the *Wamakaskan Oyate* and *Zintkala Oyate* to the South, the *Wanbli Oyate* took flight to the skies, and the *Maka Wamakaskan Oyate* disappeared into the ground below.

The *Wanbli Gleska* and I returned to my *Hanbleceya* spot on *Mato Paha*. We thanked *Ina Maka* for allowing us to see the Great Animal and Bird Blessing and expressed our deep appreciation.

I made special prayers of gratitude and thankfulness to *Mato Paha* for all that She had shown me. I thanked Her for supporting me during my *Hanbleceya*. I lifted my *Canunpa Wakan* to Her and humbly prayed out of deep respect. *Mato Paha* was truly where the presence of *Ina Maka* was the strongest.

The *Wanbli Gleska* stayed with me as I said my prayers to *Ina Maka*.

"Never forget, *Zintkala Zi Win,* never forget. Very few ever see a sacred ceremony uniting Mother Earth with Father Sky. Humans usually are not part of a ceremony for worshipping animals and birds who make their home on the planet. *Wakan Tanka has* showed you for a reason."

"*Wopila, wopila,*" I humbly replied.

"Never forget. Never forget."

The *Wanbli Gleska* lifted himself in the air. I watched him soar for a while until he was out of sight.

The Great Animal and Bird Blessing by Mother Earth and Father Sky was something I would never forget. The vision of it was miraculous. It was received with such profound humility by the animals and birds that it would be an example for me to follow the rest of my days.

I prayed, holding my *Canunpa Wakan,* that perhaps one day we humans could appear for blessings from Mother Earth and Father Sky at *Mato Paha.*

35

WHEN THE MOTHER

Gives Her blessing
Sacred blue light
From a mountain core
Erupts in waves
Of peaceful vibrations
And joins Father Sky
To love all creation.

The beautiful blue volcanic plumes from the core of *Mato Paha* remained in my heart and mind. I replayed the union of Father Sky with Mother Earth and the powerful love they had sent, which swept over us like magnificent waves of energy. I memorized every detail of the Great Animal and Bird Blessing, so my soul would never forget.

I held my *Canunpa Wakan* and thanked *Ina Maka* for the vision of sacred reverence She had given me. I promised never to forget and prayed all humans in the coming time would be present to also receive Her loving and peaceful blessing.

The *Wanbli Gleska* broke the stillness and sounded from the sky. He circled me, calling, and then landed.

"*Ina Maka* is very present here at *Mato Paha*," he began. "There are other sacred mountains in distant lands, but *Mato Paha* is one of the most *wakan* (sacred) and very rare. *Ina Maka* expresses Her beauty everywhere on the planet, but here She sends Her most precious blessings.

"You've seen a vision in the future when *Ina Maka* will bless the *Wamakaskan Oyate* and *Zintkala Oyate* at *Mato Paha*. She has given a Great Animal and Bird Blessing in the past, but we *wanbli* (eagles) have not seen one in a long, long time.

"Your people, the *Lakota Oyate*, have held many Sun Dances at the feet of *Mato Paha*. The people have been blessed as they danced by *Ina Maka* in the same way the animals and birds were blessed in your vision. In the coming time, perhaps humans will again see the sacred blue plumes of blessings from *Ina Maka*.

"The timing of Her beautiful blessings is not predictable. As you were shown in your vision, the *wamakaskan* and *zintkala* knew when the blessing was to occur, and so arrived in time to receive it. We *wanbli* knew ahead of time and will continue to hear Her calling of the blessing in the future. She sends more blessings when She is prayed to and shown respect. We have lived and flown around *Mato Paha* from when time began and felt *Ina Maka's* powerful presence there. We love *Ina Maka* beyond what we can express.

"We love *Paha Sapa* (Black Hills) in all its entirety. The hills are very *wakan* and grow the most consecrated *pejuta*. *Paha Sapa* is hallowed ground and the ancient home to many species of plants and animals including human *Lakota*.

"There is a time coming very soon when the *Lakota* will not be allowed to go to *Mato Paha* for prayer and ceremonies. None of the tribes will be allowed to appear at *Mato Paha*. The *wasicu* will invade all of *Paha Sapa*, including *Mato Paha*, and occupy your lands."

The words of the *Wanbli Gleska* were stated quietly, but I heard them like a mighty force of harm hurled at me. I knew not to question or cry out, but I felt the pain like stabs to my heart. My people would be devastated to lose all of *Paha Sapa*, their most sacred, consecrated, and ancient lands. I couldn't imagine the damage to the people if they could not worship at *Mato Paha*. I felt shaken and uncertain.

The *Wanbli Gleska* and I sat in silence for a while. I felt his presence strongly as he quietly sent me love and peace. I knew I would have an immense responsibility to the people as a medicine woman in times of great trouble. I hoped my *Unci* would always be there to teach me, so I would know what to do.

The *Wanbli Gleska* broke the silence and changed the subject to the positive. "In the coming time and after the celestial battles, *Mato Paha* and the surrounding area will again be the place for prayer and worship of *Ina Maka*. *Itacan* and his angels will be sent by *Wakan Tanka* to help heal and restore Her. Seeing this future is part of your vision."

I felt more reassured after listening to the *Wanbli Gleska*. I had been given the highest honor of my life to see a beautiful vision of the restoration of our Earth Mother. I quickly focused on the *waste'* (good) and turned all thoughts away from any negative. *Unci* had carefully taught me to always put my attention on the *waste'*, especially after my human brain was flooded with emotions.

"Future humankind," the *Wanbli Gleska* began again, "will learn to honor *Ina Maka*, pray to Her and love Her in a way they were unable to do previously. *Itacan* and his people are master teachers who will help lead humans to a much higher level of being and blessed vibrations for a new life.

"Perhaps one day in the coming time, all *oyate* will surround *Mato Paha* for miles just like the animals and birds knew to do. Perhaps *Ina Maka* will give the people beautiful blessings of blue light while joining with Father Sky. Perhaps the *Wakiyan* will dance across the skies as Father Sky joins with Mother Earth in a divine sacred blessing for all peoples.

"These are the prophesies as shown to you, *Zintkala Zi Win*. Keep the vision deep in your heart and soul, and always concentrate on the *waste'*."

"I will," I replied respectfully and humbly. My scared emotions were fleeting and immediately gone. I sat in complete gratitude once again.

The *Wanbli Gleska* gave me waves of plentiful compassion as he continued. "We will pray and hope that before the celestial battles and the coming of *Itacan's* people, all colors of humans will protect *Mato Paha* and all of *Paha Sapa* by showing great respect and concern for the Earth Mother whose presence is concentrated in every rock, tree, plant, and animal. In the coming time, perhaps the *Lakota* will again dance the sacred Sun Dance at the feet of *Mato Paha*. We will pray for all humans to grow more loving and peaceful, and to protect and respect their most sacred Mother. We know their efforts will be rewarded with beautiful blessings of sacred blue light."

The *Wanbli Gleska* stayed beside me, and I felt his loving support as I memorized every detail of the Great Blessing and prayed in thankfulness. The part of the vision that he had brought was finished.

"Never forget, never forget," he called as he flew up into the sky and disappeared in the sun.

"*Wopila, wopila*," I called after him in deep gratitude for his help.

36

WOPILA, WOPILA
Thank you, thank you
Words expressed
From the mind
Yet the heart
Sends gratitude
Beyond a person's
Understanding
The soul celebrates
The humble human
Soaring to
Touch the sky
The gift given
Of such divine nature
It must always
Be remembered
Forever and beyond.

The day was so beautiful that the mountain seemed to sing, and I felt joyful and hopeful.

"Come, *Zintkala Zi Win,* come, come," the head *Wokcanka Tahca* called as he appeared through the trees to join me.

I followed him into the realm of visions and turned myself into a *tahca*. We flew a few miles South from *Mato Paha*. We didn't go to the ridge and the valley where we had last left *Itacan* and his Angels. Instead, we flew a mile or so East. We saw new translucent structures from the air which were built in a circle. We landed in the center of the large circle of buildings. This was a second village which *Itacan* and his Angels had built.

The *Wokcanka Tahca* and I walked among the buildings. They were made of the same translucent material as the group of buildings we had first seen. The early morning sun was reflected by beautiful beams of light and color, which danced off the structures.

The *Wokcanka Tahca* explained to me as we walked. "These new dwellings you're seeing will be for spiritual purposes like prayer, meditation, sacred medicines, and the preparation of ceremonies at *Mato Paha*. Spirits and future Earth People will prepare themselves here prior to their appearance before *Ina Maka* at *Mato Paha*. *Itacan* has taught that no other dwellings, tipis or other living arrangements must ever be located anywhere around *Mato Paha*. The Earth Mother is strong at Bear Butte Mountain and She must be respected. Reverent silence needs to be maintained for several miles around Her."

We walked to a large building that was guarded by a few of *Itacan's* people. Even though it was bigger than the other buildings it emanated peace and extreme quiet.

"This building," the *Wokcanka Tahca* continued, "is where the *Pejuta Wakan* (Sacred Medicines) are stored. Come, we'll meet *Itacan* inside."

The Leader's people knew we were coming and allowed us to enter the *pejuta* (medicine) building. Once inside, I saw rows and rows of glowing containers on endless shelves that rose to the ceiling. The round containers were made of thinner translucent material and I could see shapes of *pejuta* inside them. Each container was surrounded by white light, the same energy that was around *Itacan* and his people. I peeked closely at one of the containers without touching it. The *pejuta* inside the container also glowed with white light.

Many of *Itacan's* people tended to the *pejuta*. *Itacan* saw us, greeted us warmly, and took us on a tour of the building. Each species of *pejuta* was stored together in assigned areas. As we walked from one floor and one room to another, *Itacan* told us about each *pejuta* and how it helped and healed. The tour took a long time, and I tried to absorb everything he told us.

Itacan asked us to enter a quiet but brightly lit room and rest for a moment.

The three of us sat and quietly absorbed the lovely energy the *pejuta* sent us as we passed by each one.

"*Zintkala Zi Win*," *Itacan* spoke and turned to me. "It's important that you remember all you have seen. Always remember that we will be here to help you. The *pejuta* will be very useful to you in the future. Your people will need these medicines and you will want to know how to use them. The *pejuta* will help save them. We are here to help you."

"*Wopila, wopila*," I replied humbly.

"*Wokcanka Tahca*," *Itacan* asked gently. "Please take *Zintkala Zi Win* to the *pejuta* fields. I will meet you there."

The three of us left the bright little room, went down to the first level, and exited the building. The *Wokcanka Tahca* took to the air and I knew to follow him. We flew over fields of growing *pejuta*. Countless numbers of *Itacan's* people tended the many fields of *pejuta*. Some plants were small, and some were very large with flowers as wide as people like we had been shown before. All the *pejuta* glowed in the fields with beautiful white light around them.

We flew over multiple fields where each one grew its special *pejuta*. In field after field, I saw *Itacan's* people lovingly tending to the plants. Some fields were being harvested and I saw the *pejuta* put into the special translucent containers for storage. *Itacan* waved to us from one of the fields and motioned us to join him. We landed beside him.

"*Zintkala Zi Win,* you'll know the plants and the *pejuta* in the future," *Itacan* instructed. "See how the plants glow with white light? This is how it will be. The plants that have special *pejuta* will show themselves to you by glowing. This is how you'll find them in the wild.

"We will bring advanced *pejuta* after the great cleansing and the celestial battle. All *pejuta* glows very brightly when our people plant them and attend to them with advanced spiritual care. That is why they are more potent and healing.

"When *Ina Maka* is healthy, She has strong and healthy *pejuta* in perfect combination for any sickness that would develop in Her humans and animals on Earth. If She and Her medicines are properly cared for, She can heal all illnesses. Her natural medicines are always balanced and in perfect harmony with the universe. That's why they are very potent for healing.

In the coming time, and before the great cleansing, *Ina Maka* will not be healthy and Her plants will not be potent. This will be a sad time. Just remember what you've seen. Remember in the future, we will help Her be strong again and will create advanced *pejuta* for Her to grow.

"*Zintkala Zi Win,* look at your feet."

I looked down at my feet now planted solidly in *Itacan's* fields. My feet glowed with the same white light. I saw that my entire body glowed with the white light just like *Itacan* and his people.

"See," *Itacan* pointed around me. "You are one of my people on Earth. Now, as a young medicine woman, when you see a problem in a person who has come for your help, we will show you how to help them. The Spirits you already work with will also help you. Sometimes the person may need prayer and prayer ties. Sometimes the person will need to make changes. Sometimes *pejuta* will be used and sometimes a four-day healing in an *Inipi* Ceremony will be needed.

"You will go back to your life that is now. Remember all you have seen. Know in your heart that your vision will come true, but only *Wakan Tanka* knows when. Never question or ask the timing of your vision. Remain humble before *Wakan Tanka* in all endeavors. Remain humble before all your Spirits. They will always be there to help you and work through you to help others.

"Only a few people receive a vision like the one you were given. Do not question why you were chosen to receive the vision. Never feel that you were not worthy to receive it or that it makes you better than others because you did receive it. It does not. Just accept and be deeply grateful. Only *Wakan Tanka* knows why the vision was given to you and why now. He is not to be questioned."

"*Itacan han*," (yes Leader)," I said quietly but firmly, keeping my gaze to the ground in respect. "*Itacan han. Wopila, wopila, wopila, wopila*. I will always remember. I have placed the vision deep within my soul. I will always remember. I will always remember."

"*Waste*," *Itacan* replied. "*Waste*, *Zintkala Zi Win, waste*."

37

BETRAYED BY HUMANS

Our Earth Mother wept

How could they trample me

With so little regard?

I gave them a place to live

I am their home

I helped them through hard times

I comforted them

By doing my part

To restore the planet

And grow their food

Even when assaults came

They never hesitated to take from me

Not one eye blink did they make

They needed, and that was all that mattered

They were right to do so

Never did they recognize

Their prideful greed

I should do for them

Even if it was the last

Of everything I had to give

They took it anyway

They needed it more than me

Would they think of renewal?

Would they replace the stolen?

They judged themselves right

They judged me insignificant

Then turned their backs on me

Conservation for the Mother

Allies for the future they promised

But the betrayal came

Like stinging ice pellets from a stormy sky

Their actions threw me into weeping

Caused horrible regret in me

Triggered resentment in me

For all I had done for them

I knew never to strike back

Never to do harm to them

I could only try to balance myself

And forever pray to the Creator

That one day He would

Turn this around

And I would sing

The song of creation again.

And one day,

I would sing again.

Before I could take a breath, I was back at *Mato Paha* sitting with my *Canunpa Wakan*. The head *Wokcanka Tahca* stood next to me and gazed into my eyes.

"The new era for *Ina Maka* will be glorious," he began. "Her balance will be restored, and She will be able to once again provide for all life. *Itacan* and his people will lead humans and teach them to live in unity with their Mother. It is so beautiful and uplifting to see the vision of what is to come. Do you agree?"

"It is so wonderful to see this vision and I am very grateful to all of you," I replied enthusiastically. "Walking among the glowing plants was inspiring. I can't wait to see them in the future. And all the changes the Creator will bring. It will be magnificent."

"Have you wondered how *Ina Maka* will feel before the destruction of what is to come and the celestial battles?" asked the Deer Seer. "What will Her suffering feel like?"

"*Han*," I replied and hung my head. "I can't imagine what Her anguish and torment will be."

"Since She is a living entity," the Deer Seer continued, "She feels the same emotions as humans feel. When a part of Her is carelessly stolen, She experiences pain and torment just as any human would feel. When She cannot grow glorious crops for all life, She suffers the same frustration and disappointment as a human. When Her atmosphere is polluted, and She can no longer supply adequate oxygen for breathing, She experiences anger and resentment. When *Wakan Tanka's* creatures are shrunk in numbers and suffer extinction due to human behavior, She weeps in exasperation.

"*Ina Maka* is highly evolved and an expression of the Creator's love and generosity. She does not try to get even with humankind, strike back, nor create more havoc out of spite. She feels humans' betrayal to Her very core, but She believes in the ways of *Wakan Tanka*. She prays to *Wakan Tanka* to help Her, restore Her and heal Her.

"*Ina Maka* always prays for all the life She is responsible for. She especially prays for humans to find love, peace, and humility in their hearts. She prays that humans will become more evolved and grow to understand that they are all connected to each other and to all life on the planet.

"Compassion is the positive viewpoint She frequently calls upon to help Her deal with such aggressive, hateful, greedy behavior some humans exhibit. She calls the Creator in prayer to help Her. With the Creator's assistance, *Ina Maka* feels compassion for humans and prays they will save Her and consequently save themselves.

"Evil has its influence on the Earth and walks the path of destruction. The result is great suffering for all humans, even the ones that do pray for love, compassion, and humility. All life is connected. The more suffering that humans cause themselves, the more suffering there is on the planet. This web ensnares humans. *Ina Maka* watches them as they struggle against the suffering. She sympathizes with them, has great empathy for them, and prays for their freedom from it. She is the Creator's example of living compassion. She will not strike back or try to hurt. She will only try to balance and restore Herself.

"Because there is evil on the Earth, all humans suffer. Because they cause even more of their own problems, all humans suffer. Because wars, sicknesses, and problems of many kinds are on the Earth, all humans suffer. In the coming time, the suffering will be even greater.

"There is an important question to ask all humans walking the Earth now and in the future. Can you turn from betrayal to compassion as the Earth Mother must?"

The *Wokcanka Tahca* gazed into my eyes again.

"Can you, *Zintkala Zi Win*, turn from betrayal to compassion?"

I was too overwhelmed by the question to be able to answer. I felt slight panic as I tried to think.

"You are young and still being trained in the ways of a medicine woman by your *Unci*. Pray about compassion. Ask *Wakan Tanka* for help. Pray to know how to walk in compassion no matter what arises in your life or in those you're trying to help. Whatever befalls you, whether it's betrayal or some other challenge, turn to compassion."

"*Han, han,*" I replied.

"We all have to grow into compassion, and you will need to do the same. It isn't easy. It doesn't just come to us. We must practice compassion over and over in order to receive its grace. As you grow into a woman, I know you will be able to walk with compassion."

"*Han,*" I repeated respectfully.

The Deer Seer looked to the sky.

"Help her," he prayed. "Help her learn for the future time when she will desperately need to know."

38

THE FALLING OF soft snow
A blessing from above
A tender reminder
Of a loving Creator
Who embraces His creation
In the white of sacredness.

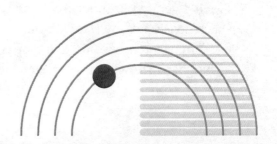

The head *Wokcanka Tahca* prayed with me a long time. I felt his silent presence throughout our time together. His prayers were incredibly strong and hopeful, always envisioning the *waste'*. I thanked him many times and felt grateful for his help and guidance.

The Deer Seer gently interrupted my prayers and whispered to me, "Never forget. Never forget."

I opened my eyes and before I could answer, he was gone and his part of the vision had ended. Soft *wa* (snow) began to fall from above. It was very gentle with just a few flakes. The *wa* did not stick to the ground and fell very peacefully. I knew it was a blessing from the Heavens, and I felt humble and grateful.

I pulled the thick buffalo robe up to cover my body with more warmth. My *Canunpa Wakan* rested in my arms in the prayer position. The four branches were around me with the prayer ties attached in a long string of colors to the four directions.

Everything about my *Hanbleceya* appeared to be the same as it had been four days prior. And yet I knew everything had changed and everything was different. I had been shown a most sacred vision and my life would be forever transformed.

It was late in the afternoon. I expected *Unci* to come walking up the hill at sunset to take me down from *Mato Paha* and my *Hanbleceya*. The Ceremony to seek a vision would soon end in an *Inipi* Ceremony.

Soft *wa* continued to fall. I smiled at the beautiful *wa* blessing. I felt a gentle reminder from the Creator to never forget the sacred vision of my *Hanbleceya*.

The *wa* gently came to a stop. I repeated in my mind all I had been shown. I memorized every detail of the vision so

I could remember. Over the *Canunpa Wakan,* I prayed in deep gratefulness to all who had shown me the vision. My heart sang with gratitude. My mind remained humbled and I stopped it from analyzing or thinking too much. I wanted to remember the vision exactly the way I had seen it. I knew not to question anything. The vision would be remembered in my *nagi* (soul) forever.

I was very grateful to *Mato Paha* during the four days of my *Hanbleceya.* She gave me warmth and calmed the winds. She gave me a vision of *Ina Maka's* distress in the coming time. She blessed my *Hanbleceya* and made it possible for Spirits to visit.

I looked up at Bear Butte Mountain's mighty core and lifted my *Canunpa Wakan* to Her in a gesture of great respect.

"*Wopila, wopila, wopila, wopila,*" I called to Her. "Thank you for letting me sit on your slope. Thank you for helping the *Wamakaskan Oyate* (Animal People), the *Zintkala Oyate* (Bird People), the *Wanagi Oyate* (Spirit People) and *Itacan* (Leader) and his people visit me. Thank you for teaching me about *Ina Maka.* Thank you for being here. Thank you for letting our people come to you with ceremonies. Thank you for helping me with my quest for a vision. Thank you."

I saw several *wanbli* fly around *Mato Paha* in a wide circle. I heard them shriek their praises as they soared up by the mountain's core. Suddenly I saw a puff of blue light emitted from *Mato Paha's* core. It was like a gentle blue *mahpiya* (cloud). The beautiful *mahpiya* of blue light rolled down the mountain toward me. It surrounded me. I immediately felt at peace as arms surrounded me in a blanket of love. I closed my eyes briefly and absorbed the divine blessing. When I opened my eyes, the blue cloud of light was gone, and *Mato Paha* was as She had been before.

Ina Maka had blessed me with Her divine light while praying at *Mato Paha.* I would always remember.

39

TO WELCOME SLEEP

Of immense peace

After an endeavor

Of remarkable value

Is to be embraced

By the Creator

In heavenly love.

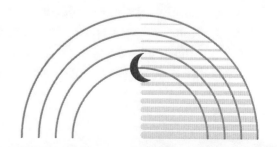

"*Zintkala Zi Win.*"

I heard my Grandmother quietly call my name as she hiked up the side of *Mato Paha*.

"*Unci.*"

She walked up to where I was sitting. *Unci Oma* and my two brothers were with her. The scout stayed behind at the camp. I was happy to see them.

"It's the end of the fourth day. Now we go down and have a hot *Inipi* Ceremony," *Unci* said cheerfully.

"*Waste*," I replied, smiling back at her.

Unci and *Unci Oma* sang sacred songs. *Unci* cut one of the leather strips that held the prayer bundles which surrounded me. It symbolized the end of my *Hanbleceya*. The Grandmothers gathered one of the buffalo robes and my brothers gathered the other one. I carefully cradled my *Canunpa Wakan*. When we had everything gathered, we all silently walked down the side of *Mato Paha*.

Everything was ready down at the bottom of the hill for an *Inipi*. The rocks were hot and ready to use. I laid my *Canunpa Wakan* on the sacred mound in front of the Sweat Lodge and went inside.

Unci led the *Inipi* Ceremony. She sang *olowan wakan* (sacred songs) and we joined her. She poured water over the hot rocks which produced purifying steam and warmed us as it touched our skin. On the third round of the *Inipi* Ceremony we smoked my *Canunpa Wakan*, which had been filled at the beginning of the *Hanbleceya* Ceremony and remained through the four days.

After four rounds of the *Inipi* Ceremony, we left the Sweat Lodge. It was dark outside and a little colder. Little stars twinkled above us, and the night was still and peaceful. *Unci* led me to her tipi, where hot coals simmered to keep us warm. We both quickly changed into dry clothes.

We joined the others in the food tipi. They had also changed into dry clothes. A cooking fire glowed in the center of the tipi, making the atmosphere lively and cheerful. The Grandmothers served stew with chunks of buffalo meat and corn and dried cherries. *Unci* told me to start with sage tea to break my fast and then slowly add a little food. She said to take my time. We all feasted, talked, and laughed happily together.

Unci Oma and the men left the food tipi after putting more wood on the fire. *Unci* said it was time for her to help me with my vision.

"*Zintkala Zi Win*," *Unci* instructed, "A teacher needs to help her student learn how to walk with a vision and how to carry it over lifetimes. Never repeat your vision to anyone else. Unless *Wakan Tanka* specifically instructs you to release your vision to the world—and He could—you are not to do so. You must guard every detail of it in your heart and soul."

I nodded in agreement before I spoke. "*Unci,* I am greatly blessed. The vision I was given was more than I could ever have imagined receiving. I am blessed beyond my understanding."

"Remember, you may tell your vision to your teacher and I am your teacher," *Unci* continued. "A teacher needs to be able to instruct a student how to carry a vision. It isn't always easy. In fact, some have found carrying a vision to be difficult. But be assured. You were ready to receive yours and you will do fine. Start at the beginning and I will help you with the interpretation."

I began at the beginning. "*Unci*, the vision told me about the future suffering of *Ina Maka*. She will get sicker and sicker due to evil and some human behaviors. She will pray and pray for help. Finally help will arrive in the form of a great cleansing and a celestial war.

"*Wakan Tanka* will send his *Ogligle Wakan* to rid *Ina Maka* of *sica* (bad, evil). The celestial battles will be fierce and will affect all forms of life on Earth. The *Wakiyan* and the *Wanbli Oyate* will be important warriors for *Ina Maka*.

"Many of the *Wamakaskan Oyate* and *Zintkala Oyate* know of this coming time and showed me what will happen during the great cleansing of evil and the celestial battles. They helped me understand how they will help *Ina Maka* in the future.

"The animal and bird people told me about sacred blessings their ancestors used to receive from *Ina Maka* at *Mato Paha*. They showed me visions of a coming time when She will again bless them. Blue light will erupt from *Mato Paha's* core.

"*Ate' Mahpiya* (Father Sky) will unite with *Ina Maka* (Mother Earth) and send immense healings of love and compassion to all those gathered.

"The *Wamakaskan Oyate* did not know of any blessings for humans when gathered at *Mato Paha* in the future. They say Her blessings happen now when our people dance the Sun Dance at the feet of *Mato Paha,* but the dance won't be allowed in the coming time.

"The *Wokcanka Tahca* taught me how to pray for *Ina Maka* in a special Ceremony and gave me a prayer for Her. They introduced me to the *Itacan* (Leader) and his people who are *Ogligle Wakan* and different from the Warrior Angels. After the celestial war, they will bring new teachings to humankind and help them start over. The Deer Seers say *Itacan's* people are very advanced in the ways of *Wakan Tanka* and will help the future Earth people rise to their true potential of love, peace, humility, and compassion." I paused to reflect and looked at *Unci,* wondering what she would say.

"*Zintkala Zi Win,*" *Unci* began. "This is a powerful vision that very few are ever blessed with. You will learn how to carry this vision in your *nagi* (soul) your entire life, and possibly into your future lives. More will be revealed to you about your vision as time goes on. We call this 'walking with a vision.' Remember, only *Wakan Tanka* knows the timing of what you have seen. You are very blessed. We are very blessed."

I told *Unci* more details of my *Hanbleceya.* At times she listened, nodded, smiled, or offered helpful interpretations. It felt good to seek my Grandmother's wisdom. I knew she would help me for as long as she walked the Earth.

I finished and realized that the first light of dawn had crept into the tipi.

"Come, come," *Unci* gently urged me. "It's time for you to rest after four days on the hill. Come, come. Tomorrow we begin our journey to join the tribe."

I went back to *Unci's* tipi. She had prepared a little bed for me, and I laid down on the waiting buffalo robe. I felt more peaceful than I could ever remember feeling in my young life. Beautiful lasting peace was in my heart and soul as I slipped into a deep gentle sleep.

40

A PRECIOUS VISION
Given to few
A solemn pledge
To walk through life
With the duty
To help others
In the way of *waste'*
The good.

The little party that had helped with my *Hanbleceya* stayed in the campsite for one extra day. We broke camp very early the next morning and headed South to join the rest of the tribe. We all rode horses and traveled as fast as we could. The Grandmothers held off the snow clouds so we would have a safe journey. We kept moving as quickly as possible, and in a few days, we arrived at our tribe's camp. They were waiting for us as planned and were ready to move. The following day, the entire tribe headed South, leaving the possibility of the blinding blizzards behind.

We *Lakota* were the peacemakers and the doctors to many other tribes. We followed the buffalo to the South in winter and back up to *Paha Sapa* in the spring. We helped many tribes along the way with spiritual teachings, healings, and ceremonies. Often, we were the only doctors for the very sick.

Unci and I had regular evening talks in our tipi with the glow of the fire to keep us warm. Different parts of the vision would come into my mind and I would ask her to help interpret. She was always very careful with how she taught me whenever the vision was the topic. She did not want me to give her too many details, because she said her only responsibility was to teach me how to carry the vision. The full responsibility of carrying the vision was mine, and I was to walk in humility and in praise of *Wakan Tanka* with the vision in my heart and soul every day of my life. She told me I would grow with the vision over my lifetime and forever.

One night in our tipi, I asked her about all the spirits who had talked to me and shown me the coming time. "These spirits from the other side," *Unci* began, "Will always stay with you, *Zintkala*

Zi Win. When spirits appear to you during your *Hanbleceya*, they are saying to you that they will walk with you always. If it were not to be, they would not appear."

I remembered *Unci* teaching me about spirits appearing and staying for one's lifetime and beyond. I had been taught these facts. Now I felt the spirits' presence fully and deeply in my soul. I felt humbled and grateful. I knew if I kept praying for guidance they would give me answers. They would teach me how to walk with them and how to help others through them.

As the weeks of winter rolled on and we traveled to help other tribes, I realized *Unci* gave me my own patients to treat. It began slowly at first with young people who could talk easier to me because I was also young. Previously I had been *Unci's* helper as she taught me how to walk as a medicine woman. Now she was giving me more responsibility. I knew it was because I had passed her test during my *Hanbleceya*. I felt honored to have gained her trust.

As time went on, she gave me more patients to treat by myself. People of all ages and circumstances reached out to me. I counseled them, taught them how to make tobacco prayer ties, prayed for them with the *Canunpa Wakan,* and healed them in *Inipi* Ceremonies. I was happy to help *Unci* because she had always tried to help more people than was sometimes realistic.

One day, *Unci Oma* sat with me when *Unci* wasn't with us. We laughed and kidded each other as we often did. We enjoyed keeping things light and cheerful.

Unci Oma asked me, "How do you like being a full medicine woman all on your own?"

I stammered for a few seconds and replied, "A full medicine woman on my own? I don't think I've reached that height yet."

"You have reached that height, *Zintkala Zi Win.*"

"I know I've been doing healings by myself, but I still want to work with *Unci* and have so much more to learn from her."

"You will learn more from your *Unci*. But you also need to establish confidence, so you can do all healings necessary by yourself," she insisted.

"I understand," I replied, "And *Unci* will help me gain confidence."

"You need to help the medicine woman in you grow with more self-reliance. Only you can do that."

I nodded my agreement. I felt slightly bewildered about what she was telling me. It seemed like she wanted to change things between me and *Unci*.

"How old are you, *Zintkala Zi Win?*" she asked.

"I've seen sixteen winters," I replied, knowing she knew my age.

"How old do you think your *Unci* is?"

"I don't know," I replied, embarrassed.

"She never wanted you to know her age," she informed me tenderly. "*Unci* needed to be both Mother and Grandmother to you when she first brought you to her tipi as a little toddler. She wanted you to think she was younger than she really was."

"But *Unci* keeps up with you," I replied, surprised by what they had told me. "She can't be much older than you, and you both get around like young people. Everyone says the two of you are so amazing."

"*Unci* is much older than me. She is now very elderly."

I hung my head, not knowing for sure what she was trying to tell me.

"I am not trying to frighten you, *Zintkala Zi Win*. I love you and your *Unci*.

"I want you to help her as much as possible while she's still with us. We all want you to walk as your own medicine woman and be fully responsible. You are ready. You will help *Unci* the most when she sees you take on the full obligation of a practicing medicine woman. This will be the most loving gift to give back to her. You could not give her anything more precious."

I realized the message she was sending me. I had many emotions. I never wanted to be without *Unci* and I felt very sad. I felt a little dazed by what she had told me. I hadn't realized my Grandmother was elderly. She was always the way she was, and I relied on her for everything.

"It's all good. *Unci* is still thriving. *Wakan Tanka* is merciful and loving."

Unci Oma calmed me down, and I saw her message more clearly. I would need to become like *Unci* as much as I could. Perhaps my Grandmother was one of the reasons the vision was given to me as a young person. I knew I would forever walk with the vision and the spirits, and they in turn would help me with the healings.

I turned to *Unci Oma*, "I love *Unci* beyond words. I will take the responsibility to walk in the medicine way as she walks. I want to help her. She has forever changed my life and I will honor her by becoming the medicine woman she trained me to be."

"*Waste', waste'*," *Unci Oma* whispered to me as we hugged in support of each other.

41

EVIL ON EARTH

Ready to infect

When called

First with negativity

Then demonic possession

Tempting humans

With power

And more power

Until the demon

Takes over

Another soul.

A few months passed, and we were still a little South and out of the worst of winter. It had been a winter of many snows with not much cold. *Unci* took advantage of the quiet of the weather to further instruct me in carrying my vision. I loved all moments with *Unci,* but I would especially remember the frosty time of the several moons that followed my *Hanbleceya.* I thought about her careful instructions, her gentle support, and her lovely patience.

I grew in confidence with the vision and held it deeply in my soul as *Unci* instructed. I learned to believe in it deeply and not question it, judge it or have any fear toward it. The Creator's way would be revealed in time. My faith and belief in the vision became very strong that winter with *Unci's* guidance.

Winter slowly ebbed into the warmth of spring. I was excited to see the new colors of yellow, purple, and green shoot up from the Earth. The *Wakiyan* returned and their energy brought Mother Earth back to life with their lightning strikes and plentiful rains.

Our tribe followed the buffalo back toward the North and our beloved *Paha Sapa.* The journey was good. We made many stops along the way to help tribes with their doctoring and ceremonies.

I had conducted several healings during the winter months just like *Unci* had taught me to do. I discovered *Unci Oma* was wiser than I had imagined. The more healings I did on my own, the more I developed confidence and self-reliance. She said it would be that way. My spirits were with me during the healings and I learned to have complete faith and trust in their support. I still asked *Unci* when I was unsure, but I tried not to burden her or worry her. I had noticed that she seemed to tire more easily and often walked with a limp.

The sacred vision I had been given during my *Hanbleceya* was always with me. Deeper understanding of different parts of the vision would appear to me seemingly from nowhere. It didn't matter what I was doing. I could be simply walking or completing a task, and new perceptions of the vision would flood my consciousness. *Unci* told me the deep-seated meaning of the vision would reveal itself over my entire lifetime. I learned to remain humble and grateful when a new meaning of the vision showed itself to me. I immediately prayed with my *Canunpa Wakan* and thanked the Creator.

On one of our stops, I was faced with a challenging healing that I knew was beyond my training. Several members of one family asked me for my help. They were suddenly ill all at the same time. Each one had different health issues, but the diseases had developed within a very short interval. *Unci* had trained me well, and I knew the next question to ask them.

"Has anyone in your family recently died?"

"*Han* (yes)," replied an older woman who seemed to be the sickest. "But how could you know?"

I replied gently. "When several members of a family are afflicted at the same time, it often means there has been a recent death. The one who has passed is usually angry over some perceived injustice and is trying to get back at certain members of the family from the other side."

The family remained silent, trying to understand what I had just said.

"It doesn't necessarily mean the deceased one is bad. He or she is usually the same on the other side as they were on the Earth plane before this happened. Sometimes they had a troubled life. Often their death is unexpected or tragic. Does any of this make sense regarding your family member?"

A young man in the family spoke first. "It makes sense. My Cousin is the one who died. He was my age and we grew up playing together. He died in a knife fight with another young man. It was an accident."

"I'm sad to hear this," I replied respectfully.

The Cousin continued. "His Mother died when he was little, and it had a bad effect on him." He gestured to the older, sicker woman standing beside him. "Auntie has been his Mother since she came to live with his Father. But he hated her and blamed her when things went wrong. As he grew up, his anger got worse. He always thought others were trying to do him harm. He would get furious and swear to get even."

"Do you all agree?" I asked.

They did.

"Who is the sickest right now?" I asked. "We will need to do one healing at a time."

They replied in unison, "Auntie."

Auntie further explained, "I can't keep food down. My stomach is upset all the time. I have pain and nausea. I've had stomach problems before, but I was given a medicine by your people and it hasn't been a problem. Now it's much worse. And I did get sick a few weeks after my stepson's death."

"This kind of situation is one our tribe does know how to handle and turn around," I explained to them with great empathy.

"*Waste'*," they replied, relieved.

"I want to discuss your situation with the tribe. How many of you are affected?"

Five held up their hands, including the Auntie and the Cousin.

"The tribe will help you while we're here." I told them.

The family and I parted, and I went to ask *Unci* for her advice. I had been *Unci's* helper during healings like this, but had never conducted one myself. This situation was very serious.

I found *Unci* resting quietly outside our tipi. I told her about the family and their situation with their dead young relative. She praised me for handling the family in a good way. Then she got up and said she was going to talk to our Chief who was an advanced medicine man.

Within a day, arrangements had been made for the family. Several medicine people would participate with different family members. Two more sweat lodges were quickly built, and the preparations were underway for the healings.

Our Chief asked me to be his helper during the four-day healing for Auntie. I was very honored and happy to assist him. *Unci* told me to pay careful attention to how he did the healing, because he was very advanced with healings concerning negative entities and demons.

The four-day healing done in an *Inipi* Ceremony was intense and severe. It strained the medicine people. After the first day of the sweat lodges, they realized they were dealing with a demon and that it could be rough.

At times during the *Inipi* Ceremonies for Auntie, I could see the young man who had died and the demon who possessed him. I knew to pay no attention to the evil, even though I could see it. I did not allow the images to permeate my being.

Our Chief asked the spirits to remove the demon who had infested the young man since childhood. I saw the Chief's spirits come in and remove the demon. The Chief prayed that the young man be free to move to the spirit world and beyond the Earth plane. He asked his spirits to escort the young man to a place of safety where he could get help. The spirits took the young man away. I saw he would now get help for his soul and compassion from the spirits.

After the four days of healing for the Auntie, she felt much better. She was doctored with medicine for her stomach and she had color back in her face. She carefully ate as the Chief directed without any discomfort or pain in her stomach.

The rest of the family had the same positive outcome. The medicine people thanked the spirits for their help and we felt humble and grateful that this very dangerous situation had turned around for the better.

After the feast and the celebration of the healings, I went back to the tipi I shared with *Unci*. She had already returned and was resting.

"The Chief tells me he was very impressed with you as his helper," she began. "He said most people could not face a demon without getting very afraid or running away. He said your prayers were strong and you stood your ground."

"*Wopila, Unci,*" I replied smiling. "You taught me to be strong and pray deeply for *Wakan Tanka's* help in all things."

She replied, smiling back, "Yes, I did. I am very grateful for you today. A Grandmother likes to feel proud occasionally." She chuckled and kissed me on the cheek.

42

WAKAN TANKA WAITS

For humans
He waits for them
To help save
Mother Earth
He waits for them
To turn away
And fight evil
Wakan Tanka waits
Patiently
For His children
To help their own
Earth Mother
Wakan Tanka waits
And waits.

The following morning after the demon healing, I woke up very early just as the sun's rays first rose in the sky. *Unci* was still sleeping, and I dressed and gathered my things very quietly.

I put my *Canunpa Wakan* in a leather satchel so I could easily carry it. I set out to hike up a hill covered in pine trees. It was a little way from our tipis.

I wanted to be alone and pray. The vision during my *Hanbleceya* came back to me. Throughout the night I was given more insight about the evil that would permeate the Earth in the coming time. The advanced medicine healers could heal people from demons now, but I wondered if that would be possible in the future time of my vision.

I hiked for a while and felt the sun warming the day. Spring was in full bloom with a beautiful blue sky and budding wild flowers. I found a little clearing among the pine trees where I could sit in privacy and pray.

I pulled out a small blanket I had brought with me and put it on the ground. I smudged myself and the area around me with sage. I filled the *Canunpa Wakan* and prayed. I sang sacred songs as I waited.

As I stayed in prayer and song, a figure appeared before me. She was dressed in white buckskins. She had long dark hair and an aura of white was all around Her. I recognized Her immediately. It was *Ptesan Win*. She stood before me and sent rays of white light. I humbly thanked Her.

"You have prayed regarding your vision," She began.

I nodded, not looking in Her eyes.

"Your vision foresees a wonderful new era, one that *Wakan Tanka* has ruled needs to take place at a certain time in Mother

Earth's manifestation of the good. Before the new era is timed to take place, evil will have overtaken the planet. *Ina Maka* will be very ill and in need of great healing.

"Your vision has shown you that humankind will be partly responsible. They will have enabled evil to take over because humans will have allowed it. Many humans will have invited it into their lives. Even the medicine people will no longer be able to rid it from humans. Evil is smart and cunning and can manipulate people to let it in. Humans didn't bring evil here, but the infection of evil over most people in the coming time will be very regrettable. The transition to the beautiful new era will be much more difficult for every living creature because evil will have permeated the planet.

"Long ago *Wakan Tanka* asked me, *Ptesan Win,* to bring the *Canunpa Wakan* to the Earth Planet and teach the people a humble way to walk on the Earth and praise their Creator. *Wakan Tanka's* ways are peaceful, loving and in balance with creation. They do no harm. They consider *Ina Maka* and all Her creatures and plants. They respect Father Sky with His sunshine and rains. They teach humankind to consider the consequences of all their actions for seven generations to follow. The ways of the Creator are humble and compassionate. They show honor and respect for all life.

"*Wakan Tanka* has taught that we are all related, *Mitakuye Oyasin.* We are related to each other and to all forms of life no matter how small or how big. Mother Earth and Father Sky are our relatives. We are related to the lightning, the animals, the birds, the plants, and the tiniest bug.

"Humankind can turn to the *Canunpa Wakan* and me, *Ptesan Win,* as a teacher and an example of how to go forward in a good way honoring all life.

"If humans do not find a way to come together, fight evil, and continue to let it grow, then the vision that was given to you, *Zintkala Zi Win,* of the coming time will come into reality. *Wakan Tanka* does not want to act against His people, but He cannot allow evil to completely overtake the good for the sake of all life on the planet.

"Humans will know about the destruction in the coming time deep down in their hearts. They will sense it and will know. They can decide to ignore their own innate warnings or act together to keep evil away. *Wakan Tanka* will wait for a change from human beings because He is a loving Creator. He will wait, but He will want a transformation that includes all the people of Earth.

"The vision has told you that *Wakan Tanka* is patiently waiting. He will wait for His beloved and blessed human beings to turn things around. He will wait for them to ask for help. He will provide them with all occasions to change. He will send every form of help to them, so they can act in a good way. He will wait. He will wait some more. He will wait for humans again and again. He will give them every opportunity.

"He will wait until He can no longer wait. And then He will unleash the great cleansing of evil and the celestial war. It will happen, but only in His time."

Ptesan Win sent wonderful rays of sacred white light to me and then vanished. I felt deep gratitude and humbly thanked Her. Her appearance over the *Canunpa Wakan* gave me more understanding of the vision I had been given on my *Hanbleceya*. *Wakan Tanka* was a loving, patient Creator who wanted the best for His creation. He gave them free will so they could grow and mature their own souls while on Earth. He wanted His beautiful new vision for *Ina Maka* to materialize. He wanted all His creation to walk in the beautiful, loving, compassionate time that He had created for them in the future.

I now understood more clearly why *Unci* told me the vision would walk with me the rest of my life and possibly into a future life. I also realized I would be given more clarity over time.

I packed up my things and walked down from the little pine-tree covered hill. I joined *Unci* outside our tipi.

She rushed up to me. "You're here," she exclaimed, out of breath. "The tribe is leaving today. Several of the men are coming soon to help us with the tipi."

"Don't worry, *Unci*," I replied, assuring her. "I'll be a tornado and get us ready like a big gust of wind."

She laughed as I acted out being a tornado.

Unci Oma joined in the laughter. We all loved a good laugh. Humor was one of our medicines.

43

A CALL TO women
From the Calf Woman
To help Mother Earth
Stand up together
Fight for Her
Protect Her
Respect Her
She is your home
Let Her flourish
And provide for all
Women of the world
Help your Earth Mother.

everal weeks of travel passed. We finally arrived back in *Paha Sapa* and set up camp near *Mato Paha*. The tribe would soon be participating in the *Hanbleceya* (Vision Quests) and the *Wiwanyang Wacipi* (Sun Dances).

Unci and I loved springtime in the Black Hills. The rains were more plentiful, and the hills were a blanket of bright green. Little wild flowers flashed brilliant color on various hillsides. We listened for the sound the pine trees made when gusts of wind blew through them. Their gentle noises were enchanting, mysterious, and mesmerizing.

Unci, Unci Oma, and I had a few days to get settled, and then we made our usual plans to gather the Spring medicines. We decided we would go out on the land the following morning. We set out all our baskets and tools in preparation.

Unci asked me to bring my *Canunpa Wakan.*

"*Zintkala Zi Win,*" she began, "You've told me you want to dedicate your life to help *Ina Maka* and continue your healings for others."

"*Han, Unci,*" I replied.

"This is good," she continued. "We'll smoke your *Canunpa Wakan* while we're out gathering medicines and pray about it. I know a good place to say our prayers."

I was happy *Unci* and *Unci Oma* would pray with me. Their prayers were strong, and I looked forward to the next day.

Early morning arrived in a gentle calm and we left camp. *Unci* led us to the place she knew we could pray in peace. She said we would do our prayers first and then find the medicines.

We laid down a large blanket, and *Unci* burned sage to purify the little area around us before prayers. We used sage to bless each of us. We said our prayers for *Ina Maka*, sang sacred songs, and smoked my *Canunpa Wakan*.

The three of us were seers and medicine women. We saw *Ptesan Win* appear and walk toward us. She was clothed in white and was engulfed in beautiful rays of luminous light.

"I see three spiritual women before me," She began. "This is very good. As women, you are part of Mother Earth. The men are part of Father Sky. It is the way of *Wakan Tanka*. It will be necessary in the coming time for the women to lead the way to protect *Ina Maka*. The women must be strong and help the Mother. The men will follow you, but they are of Father Sky and cannot feel the hurt of the Earth Mother like you can.

"My message to you as women is one of hope. Humans can turn things around in the coming time when *Ina Maka* is threatened. When women stand together and become the leaders to save *Ina Maka*, it can happen. She can be saved before the new era that is to come. If She is helped at that time, all of Creation will have an easier time transitioning into the new way that *Wakan Tanka* has created for the future.

"*Zintkala Zi Win,* the vision given to you during your *Hanbleceya* has caused a deep commitment in you to help *Ina Maka* in the coming time. This is very good. Teach the women to devote themselves to help *Ina Maka* in whatever ways they are able. Help them to stand together. Ask them if they see Her distress. Ask them if they feel Her pain. Ask them if they cry for their Earth Mother. Numerous women will be the first to answer. 'I do. And I do. And I do. And we do. We all do. All of us women do.' And when the women answer together and stand up, the men will fight for the Mother too."

The three of us were moved to tears. Her instructions were so passionate and reasonable that we knew we must follow and dedicate our lives to Her request.

"Who cries for Mother Earth? I do, *Zintkala Zi Win,* I cry for *Ina Maka*. I dedicate my life to the Earth Mother," I prayed silently to Her.

"Help the women," *Ptesan Win* appealed to us. "Teach them and help them. Remember, *Wakan Tanka* will wait as long as possible to intercede. Teach the women so they know how to stand up and protect Mother Earth."

Ptesan Win receded into the luminous white light and was gone.

"*Wopila, wopila, wopila, wopila*," we called after Her.

We stood up slowly and gathered our belongings to go pick medicines. We were quiet and respectful of *Ptesan Win's* appearance and to each other's thoughts and feelings. We walked out of the little clump of trees where we had been praying.

I looked across the way to a clearing and saw all my spirits lined up next to several magnificent pine trees. I was happy when I saw them. Suddenly I saw *Unci* join them. I was puzzled and turned my head to see her standing next to me in human form. I turned back to the spirits and saw her again in spirit form. She was with my spirits smiling and happy but standing next to me in human form all at the same time.

In a flash, I realized the spirits were telling me that *Unci* would be joining them soon. I knew then that Grandmother would be leaving her body. No longer to walk on the Earth. No longer to be with me. No longer to teach me and guide me.

I felt sudden sadness and I couldn't catch my breath. An elder once told me that no one is ever prepared for the death of a loved one even if they know it's coming. I wanted to cry out. "No, not now. Wait a little while. I'm still young. You're the only parent I've ever really known."

I tried to quiet my emotions and remained silent, not wanting to upset *Unci*. I wondered if she knew. I wondered how long it would be, even though I knew not to question the Creator's ways with the question of when. Many thoughts raced through my mind.

In seconds, my entire childhood flashed before me as I remembered my beloved *Unci* always beside me and devoted to me. I remembered her love for me, and her steady guidance in teaching me to be a medicine woman.

I turned to look at her standing next to me. For the first time, I realized how elderly she was. I wondered if she wanted to go now. I knew she was always in pain with her hip and had trouble walking. Suddenly I felt a little selfish. I could see that it was time for her to go to the other side. I knew and deeply believed that she would stay with me as long as she possibly could, but I also knew that she deserved to suffer no more.

In that instant, I realized a part of me had not yet grown up. I knew what to do. I needed to stand up and fully become the medicine woman *Unci* had trained me to be. I needed to grow up completely. I could no longer hide behind my youth or lack of experience. I would get the experience. I carried within me the power of a vision to help the people. Everything *Unci* had put into me I now needed to give back to our people.

A deep resolve welled up in me. I could see my purpose in life laid out before me. I would walk the way of a medicine woman and fight for *Ina Maka*. I knew this was my duty in life, but I hadn't realized the depth of commitment it would take until that moment. I immediately placed the responsibility and devotion of the medicine work deep within my soul.

"This will be my life's work starting now," I vowed out loud so that all could hear. "I will dedicate my life to being a medicine woman in every way, and that will include praying and fighting for the healing of *Ina Maka*."

My spirits were still gathered by the pine trees. I looked directly at them as I made the vow.

"*Waste*'," they replied, "*lila waste*'. Know that one day you will give your vision to the people, and to the world. *Wakan Tanka* has now willed it. Remember, He is the only one who knows when."

My two Grandmothers heard the pronouncement from me and the reply from the spirits. They listened reverently and acknowledged my firm commitment.

Unci turned to face me and lovingly took my hands in hers.

"My Granddaughter," she said quietly, "I am so proud of you. You will be a wonderful blessing to the people. I want you to realize I will always be with you. Remember."

I put my arm around *Unci* and embraced her. She laid her head on my shoulder.

"I will always be with you," she repeated. "Always."

THE END

GLOSSARY OF *LAKOTA* WORDS USED

PRONUNCIATION GUIDE
A like ball
E like French words sauté or soufflé
I like gasoline
O like hope
U like prune

A

Apetu Waste' (a-pe'-tu wah-shtay') Good Day
Ate' (a-tay') Father
Ate' Wakan Tanka (a-tay' wa-kan' tan-ka') Father Great Spirit
Ate' Mahpiya (a-tay' mah-pee'-yah) Father Sky

C

Canli Wapahta (chun-lee' wa-pah'-ta) Tobacco Ties or Prayer Ties
Cansasa (chun-sha'-sha) Red Willow Bark
Cante (chun-tay') Heart
Canunpa Wakan (cha-nun'-pa wa-kan') Sacred Pipe

G

Gleska (glesh-kah') Spotted

H

Hanbleceya (hahn-blay'-chee-yah) Vision Quest
Han (hahn) Yes [Female]
Hehaka (hay-hah'-kah) Elk
Hehaka Oyate (hay-hah'-kah oh-yah'-tay) Elk People or Elk Nation
Hihanni Waste' (hee-hahn'-nee wash-tay') Good Morning
Hiya (hee-ye'ah) No
Hogan (hoh-ghan') Fish

I

Ina (ee-nah') Mother
Ina Maka (ee-nah' mah-kah') Mother Earth
Inipi (ee-nee'-pee) Sweat Lodge
Itacan (ee-tah'-cha) Leader

K

Kimimila (kee-mee'-mee-lah) Butterfly

L

Lakota (lah-koh'-tah) The Friendly
Lakota Oyate (lah-koh'-tah oh-yah'-tay) Lakota People or Lakota Nation
Lila Waste' (lee'-lah wash-tay') Very Good

M

Maka (mah-kah') Earth
Maka Oyate (mah-kah' oh-yah'-tay) Earth People
Maka Wamakaskan Oyate (mah-kah' wah-mah'-kah-shkah oh-yah'-tay) Earth Animal People
Mato Paha (mah-toh' pah-hah') Bear Butte Mountain
Mahpiya (mah-pee'yah) Cloud
Matanyan (mah-tah'-yahn) I am fine.
Mitakuye Oyasin (Mee-tak'-koo-yay oh-yah'-see) All My Relations

N

Nagi (nah-ghee') Soul
Nagi Wakan (nah-ghee' wak-khan') Sacred Spirits

O

Ogligle (og-lig'-lay) Angel
Ogligle Wakan (og-lig'-lay wah-kahn') Sacred Angel
Oyate (oh-yah'-tay) People or Nation
Olowan (oh-loh'-wahn) Song
Olowan Wakan (oh-loh'-wahn wah-kahn') Sacred Song

P

Paha Sapa (pah-hah' sah-pah') Black Hills
Pejihota (peh-zjee-hoh'-tah) Sage
Pejuta (peh-zjue'-tah) Medicine

Pejuta Wakan (peh-zjue'tah wah-kahn') Sacred Medicine

Pilamaya (pee-lah'-mah-yah) Thank You

Ptesan Win (ptay'-san wee) White Buffalo Calf Woman

S

Sica (shee'-chah) Bad, Evil

Ska (shkah) White

Sunkawakan (shun'-ka wah-kahn') Horse

Sunkawakan Oyate (shu'-ka'-wah-kahn' oh-yah'-tay) Horse People

T

Tahca (tah-gchah') Deer

Tahca Oyate (tah-gchah' oh-yah'-tay) Deer People

Tajuska (ta-ju'-ska) Ant

Tajuska Oyate (ta-ju'-ska oh-yah'-tay) Ant People

Tatanka (tah-than'-kah) Buffalo

Tatanka Oyate (tah-than'-kah oh-yah'-tay) Buffalo People or Nation

Tatanka Ska (tah-than'-kah shkah) White Buffalo

Tate' (tah-tay') Wind

Tonituka he (ton'-nee-tu-ka hay) How are you?

Tunkasila (tun-kah'-shee-la) Grandfather Spirits

U

Unci (un-chee') Grandmother

Unci Oma (un-chee' oh-ma') Grandmother Other

Unci Makata (un-chee' ma-ka'-ta) Grandmother Spirits

W

Wa (wah) Snow

Wabluska (wah-blue'-shkah) Insect

Wabluska Oyate (wah-blue'-shkah oh-yah'-tay) Insect People

Wahinheya (wah-hee'-hay-yah) Mole

Wahinheya Oyate (wah-hee'hay-yah oh-yah'-tay) Mole People

Wakan (wah-kahn') Sacred

Wakan Tanka (wah-kahn' tahn-kah') Great Spirit, Creator, God

Wakiyan (wah-kee'-yahn) Lightning/Thunder Beings

Wamakaskan (wah-mah'-kah-shkah) Animal

Wanagi (wah-nah'-gee) Spirit

Wanagi Oyate (wah-nah'-gee oh-yah'-tay) Spirit People

Wanagi Wakan (wah-nah'-gee wah-kahn') Sacred Spirit
Wanbli (wan-blee') Eagle
Wanbli Gleska (wan-blee' glesh-kah') Spotted Eagle
Wanbli Oyate (wan-blee' oh-yah'-tay) Eagle People
Wasicu (wah-shee'-chue) White Man
Waste' (wah-shtay') Good
Wiwanyang Wacipi (wee-wahn'-yahn wa-chee'-pee) Sun Dance
Wokcanka (wo'-kcan-ka) Seer
Wokcanka Tahca (wo'-kcan-ka tah'-gchah) Deer Seer
Wolakota (wo'-lah-koh'-tah) Peaceful
Wopila (wo'-pee-la) Thank You

Z

Zi (zee) Yellow
Zintkala (zjee-kah'-lah) Bird
Zintkala Oyate (zjee-kah'-lah oh-yah'-tay) Bird People
Zintkala Zi Win (zjee-kah'-lah zee wee) Yellow Bird Woman

ACKNOWLEDGMENTS

I would like to thank my family, Conrad, Christina, and Olivia, for their help and loving support. You forever fill my heart with joy.

With respect and humility, I thank the Lakota people. I am forever appreciative and very grateful to have learned a little of your beautiful, spiritual ways. They have provided inspiration, compassion, and miraculous healing for many people, including me. *Wopila.*

I thank my many teachers for their patience and persistence turning a skeptical seeker into a true believer.

I'd like to thank the many people who have helped me with the book. Chief Reginald Left Hand Bull for his gentle encouragement and his patient help with the Lakota language. Charles Trimble for believing in me and going the extra step to write a foreword. I thank Jerome A. Greene for his help in checking historical facts, and his kind comments. And I'd like to thank Walt and Linda Duda for their encouragement and friendship.

I want to acknowledge the great work of Lisa Pelto, who edited the book and steered me to an improved manuscript, and also to thank Lisa and her wonderful staff at Concierge Marketing for all their help in the publication of this book.

And lastly, I would like to thank "vision", which is an ability in all people, and a beacon of light shining brightly over us all as we walk our various paths to the good.

ABOUT THE AUTHOR

I wanted to write a book that would help Mother Earth. I was inspired by participating in Lakota Sweat Lodges, going on the hill to do Vision Quests, and attending and dancing in Sun Dances. These beautiful ways of the Lakota inspired me to tell the story of seeing Mother Earth from the Spirits', Animals', and Mother Earth's perspective. My hope for the book was that it would help turn hearts from apathy to compassion to action for our Earth Mother.

I grew up in the Black Hills of South Dakota and wandered the hills and cliffs when I was a young child. As long as I took my dog, my parents let me go. Those were the most inspirational of times. The pine trees spoke to me, the breezes whispered words of encouragement, the clouds sent me shapes with messages, and the deer came near and touched my heart.

I left the Black Hills, went to college, married, had children, and started my career first in broadcasting and then in advertising. I began as a copywriter and expanded from there. Like most people, I had many trials in my life. Some were very traumatic. These difficulties led me to become a seeker of truth and took me to places across the planet.

It wasn't until I went back home to the people of Western South Dakota that I found myself again. I realized that vision was one of the most beautiful gifts from the Creator, and that I would forever be grateful for any tiny glimpses I was allowed to see.

After a long time, I reunited my grown-up and often wounded self with the child of inspiration and vision who had wandered Mother Earth's beautiful hills and cliffs with her collie dog, Laddie, always by her side.